The Riddle of the Russian Gold

by G. H. Teed

A Tale of Thrilling Detective Adventure, introducing Dr. Huxton Rymer.

From the Sexton Blake Library magazine dated 31 Dec. 1926. No. 73 (2nd Series).

Stillwoods Edition, 2019.

Stillwoods.Blogspot.Ca

Catalogue Information:
Title: The Riddle of the Russian Gold
Author: G. H. Teed (1886-1938)
First Published: Sexton Blake Library magazine dated 31 Dec. 1926. No. 73 (2nd Series).Original cover illustrated by Arthur Jones and adapted.
This Edition: Stillwoods, 2019
ISBN Canada: 978-1-988304-76-2
Blog: Stillwoods.Blogspot.Ca
Author's Blog: http://ghteed.blogspot.com/
Storefront: http://www.lulu.com/spotlight/lulubook22

Keywords: Sexton Blake, Dr. Huxton Rymer, Mary Trent, British detective fiction

Synopsis:
Unbeknownst to each other, both Sexton Blake and Dr. Huxton Rymer find themselves in search of Gold inside the new Bolshevist Russia after the revolution. As well they have been betrayed by their shipping agent.

Can either of these two get their 'assignment' completed? Can either escape? Can they cooperate?

CHAPTER 1. The Chandler of Port Said—The Mystery of the Golden Domes.

DR. HUXTON RYMER emerged from the Continental Hotel at Port Said and took his way eastwards along the waterfront. August is not the month one chooses to make a stay in Egypt and, with the exception of a few Levantine Greeks who were in port on business, Rymer was almost the sole visitor at the hotel.

Not that it was not crowded in the restaurant and on the terrace when passengers from one of the big liners homeward bound from India, Australia and the Far East came ashore for a breather; or when those who were outward bound landed to spend an hour or so among the shops and bazaars before passing through the Suez Canal, which is such a complete line of demarcation between West and East.

There was a plentiful array of craft on this hot afternoon lying off in the roadstead but most were tramps, and not since the previous day had there been an influx of transients. Therefore the streets contained few Europeans as Rymer, clad in loose pongee silk, and wearing a topee to protect his head from the ardent rays of the sun, strolled slowly along puffing appreciatively at a choice Egyptian cigarette, and casting a critical eye at the heterogeneous collection of ships off in the roadstead.

He himself had arrived only the previous day by a P. & O. liner which had already continued her voyage through the Canal, and since he had come ashore had remained almost exclusively at the Continental. One who knew Dr. Huxton Rymer might have suspected he was marking time, waiting for something to happen; and, indeed, this is exactly what he had been doing.

Just before lunch a note had been handed to him, and it was the contents of that note which had inspired him to leave the hotel early in the afternoon and take his way eastwards towards the lower native bazaar.

But he did not proceed through the bazaar proper. Instead, when he had almost reached the end of the line of wharves, just before the sandy banks narrow to the opening of the Canal, he swung to the right and followed a narrow street which seemed to be lined mostly with the blank walls of warehouses.

On the right of this street, some two hundred yards or so from the waterfront, he came to a sign which informed all and sundry that it was the business premises of one "D. Halloran, Ship Chandler."

Rymer turned in at the open door, finding himself immediately in an atmosphere which was redolent of tar and oil and paint; of the smell of new cordage and old junk. To a man who loved the sea, as did Huxton Rymer, it caused him to pause in the welcome gloom of the shop and sniff the air with pleasure; then his gaze roved over the stock which was piled in mixed heaps as if the owner had thrown everything into the first available spot as soon as it had arrived.

There were gleaming brass instruments, compasses and lamps and binnacle-tops; coils of new manila rope of every conceivable size piled side by side with kegs of nails and paint and oil; bits of spars and heaps of sails; boiler tubes and furnace doors and other weird bits of iron which only a marine engineer could have named; lanterns of all sorts swung from hooks, or were heaped up in one corner, and in a great glass case—for a wonder were various forms of chronometers.

It was well stocked as a chandlery, as indeed it had to be, for "D. Halloran" was known to every seaman who sailed the seven seas and there were few ships, large or small that had ever passed through the Canal which Halloran had not supplied in some form or other.

The only person visible was a gigantic, half-naked Nubian who was squatting behind a low counter tinkering with a battered-looking lantern. He glanced up as Rymer came in, but did not offer any form of salutation; nor did he attempt to rise.

As for Rymer, he paid no attention to the black, but picked his way between the heaps of cordage and kegs until, in the deep gloom at the back, he came to a closed door. He knocked thrice on this, and almost immediately a voice bade him enter.

Rymer pushed open the door and stepped into a small office which contained for furniture only a plain flat-topped desk, two or three chairs, and, against one wall, a couch.

A modern steel filing cabinet and a heavy safe completed the heavier fittings, and, with the exception of the litter of papers on the desk, the room was a startling contrast of neatness and order compared to the shop outside.

Seated at the desk beneath an electric fan was a man clad only in soiled white bags and singlet. He was an extraordinary looking individual; gaunt and pinched, and as yellow as Sumatra tobacco after the curing.

His poll was as bald as the bowl of a spoon, and his pale-blue, dead-looking eyes gave one the impression that the face was more of a mask than the visage of a living man.

His long nose drooped over a straggling, yellowish moustache, and down his chin was a line of brown drool from the quid of tobacco he was chewing.

He was not an attractive looking person was D. Halloran, and an ordinary visitor would have turned away a little disgusted and thinking that he was just some nonentity who had found anchorage in that evil port of the Near East.

But not so those who had lived along the shores of the Levant and had mixed sufficiently in the under circles there to catch some of the whispers that found their way along the Mediterranean. To such persons the name "D. Halloran" meant something to ponder over and to gossip about—if anyone could be found to talk, which was seldom.

For thirty years or more this strange individual had conducted his chandlery shop in Port Said. Whence he had come none knew. How he had found anchorage in that spot none could tell. But there were rumours—rumours of the most fantastic nature sometimes.

It was said that the ship chandlery business, genuine though it was, was but a blind for deep intrigues whose strings were controlled by Halloran.

There were whispers that no political plotting had taken place in Egypt in twenty-five years in which Halloran had not had a hand, and out of which he had not raked a profit.

In Alexandria and Tunis, even along the whole stretch of the North African coast, was his name known and whispered of. Up the Levantine shore—at Jaffa and on to Constantinople—it was known, and there were whispers that when the Turks drove the Greeks out of Asia Minor a few years back, it was D. Halloran who collected more profit out of that than anyone else.

There was talk of his activities down through the Red Sea, and it was even said that he had a hand in the financing of the daring desert sheik, Ibn Saud, of Nejd in his war against the Hashimite who ruled Mecca and which ended in the surrender of the holy city of the Moslems a few months ago.

Be that as it may, Ibn Saud is now king of Mecca and the whole desert country from the Persian Gulf to the Red Sea; and "D. Halloran" has recently opened up a place of business at Jeddah. Rumours in plenty there are about this strange individual but Dr.

Huxton Rymer could have told that not one half that was said approached the whole truth.

Rymer knew something more than the average person, for he had worked with Halloran in the past. Only at rare intervals did those two join forces, and then it was because Rymer was the most suitable man for a particular job.

But, in partnership with Halloran, he had always come out of the deal considerably richer than when he went in, and that is why, when he had received a code telegram in London, some ten days before, he had lost no time in leaving for Port Said.

On arriving, the previous afternoon, he had not made the mistake of going to the ship chandler's place of business. He had sent a code message from Marseilles which contained the brief information that he was sailing from that port by a certain P. and O. boat, and he knew that Halloran would communicate with him as soon as he was ready to talk business.

It had been nearly two years since those two had seen each other, but their greeting was a simple casual nod, and dropping into a chair, Rymer waited for the other to speak. When he did so his voice came with an extraordinary soft "slur," almost a whisper.

"I have something which I believe will interest you," he said slowly, "Are you free to take it on?"

"There is a little business in London, but I can shelve it if the other is worth while."

"There is four hundred thousand or more in it," answered the ship chandler, as casually as it he were speaking of a few hundreds.

"Sterling?"

"Gold bullion."

"That sounds interesting. But I take it the stuff isn't exactly lying loose ready to be picked up. Otherwise you wouldn't have sent for me."

"Quite right. I only heard of it a couple of weeks ago. It is not going to be easy. I have no plan. But I know where it is!"

"The spot?"

"Odjiska."

"The Black Sea port in the Crimea?"

"Yes."

Rymer stroked his pointed, black beard.

"That means the Bolshy gauntlet must be run, I take it? Or are they mixed up in it?"

"No. They are after it, too. They know it is in Odjiska but they don't know its exact whereabouts. Neither do I, but I will tell you the story. Ever hear of the golden-domed church at Petrovad?"

"Of course. I have seen it!"

"The covering plates on that dome were pure gold as well as the plates on the two smaller domes. I understand that by actual weight the gold was worth two hundred thousand pounds. The bullion I speak of is partly made up of those plates."

Rymer whistled softly.

"How the devil was it worked? And who managed it?"

"There was crookedness among the members of the local Soviet council. Bribery did the trick. All the plates off the domes were stripped and melted down; copper sheets were put on instead. Then all the gold vessels in the church—chalices and cups, as well as a great golden cross and the whole treasure of centuries—were also melted down. Some two tons of the pure metal, worth, as I have said, four hundred thousand or more."

"Moscow didn't get to hear of it until the job had been completed and the bullion had been shipped out of Petrovad. They acted in the usual way; sent a regiment and massacred every manjack of the local Soviet, and a hundred or so of the inhabitants as well. But that didn't get back the gold. With a three weeks' start it was well on its way to the frontier, and eventually it, reached Odjiska. There it arrived and there it is still, unless those in the plot have succeeded in getting it out, which I don't believe."

"Who was in the plot?"

"Some of the old Kerensky crowd and Royalists. It was destined for Paris as part of the war chest of the Grand Duke Nicholas. The Bolshevists are tearing their hair with rage. They are fine-tooth combing every port on the Black Sea and every ship that enters and leaves. They have discovered—or think they have discovered— that the bullion is in Odjiska, and my information is that the port is alive with Secret Service men who are trying to locate it. But there it lies, and there it will be until someone with sufficient nerve and a workable plan turns up to lift it."

"It looks like a tough nut to crack."

"It is. I have rarely seen a harder. But it is up to you. If you take it on, I shall, as usual, do the financing, and supply you with anything you need. But you will have to do the actual lifting yourself."

"The Bolshevists after it," muttered Rymer, "and I suppose the bunch who got it as far as Odjiska are still trying to figure out some scheme for getting it away."

"You can take that as a certainty."

"If this gets whispered abroad there will be others after it as well," went on Rymer. "Gold in bulk like that is enough to bring every carrion crook along the Levant into the game."

"As us. It is up to us to beat them to it."

"You are sure of your information?"

"Do I ever act when there is any doubt?"

"No, I guess you don't."

"My informant is to be depended upon. He was one of the party that brought the bullion from Petrovad. He sold the information for ready money. He lost his nerve before the caravan got to Odjiska, so he doesn't know exactly where it has been hidden, or in whose care. But he knows it is there."

"I'll have to think this over. I'll see if I can hit on something to-night. If I take it up, I suppose the usual terms?"

"Of course—one quarter to you, three-quarters to me, and I stand all the expenses. But if you decide to take it on there is no time to be lost."

"I realise that. I'll come round again to-morrow morning, if that will suit you."

"Any time between eleven and twelve."

With that Rymer rose, and, after helping himself to a cigarette from a box on the desk, gave the shipchandler a nod and made his way out.

He strolled back to the Continental by way of the waterfront, thinking deeply as he went, and then, as he stepped on to the terrace, he quickened his step and strode along between the tables until he reached one at the far end where a very pretty girl, clad in dainty white, was sitting.

It was his partner, Mary Trent.

AS Rymer sat down Mary shot him an inquiring glance. But he made a negative gesture with his head.

"Not here," he said in a low tone. "We'll take a walk later, and I'll tell you." Then, to the white-jacketed waiter: "Bring me an iced squash!"

When the long cooling drink was brought they sat talking commonplaces while Rymer sipped it, smoking a cigarette idly while he listened to Mary's account of a visit to the bazaar. But presently Rymer rose and suggested casually that they should go for a walk, so when Mary had found her parasol they started out.

"Not the bazaars," said Rymer as they went along, "the safest place to talk in this country is in the open. We'll walk past the mosque and get out on to the edge of the desert if it won't be too far for you."

"Not at all. I'd like it."

For the first part of the way they were pestered by small native boys and street mountebanks, and not least by shop keepers, but when these nuisances saw that the two Europeans ignored them as if they didn't exist, they gave it up, and by the time they reached the mosque they were alone. They passed this great building, and, cutting along an avenue of date palms, kept straight on towards the open desert.

From the edge of the town there was a stretch of about half a mile to a small clump of date palms; and it was towards the shade that Rymer led the way. Once they were clear of any chance of being overheard he pressed the end of a cigar and gazed down at Mary.

"Well my dear, old Halloran has sprung a big thing this time—if it can be pulled off. But I don't think I have ever tackled anything more difficult than this looks."

"Is it something here?"

"No. It is at a place called Odjiska, in the Crimea."

"A Russian port that would be."

"Your geography is not at fault, my dear."

"Is it near Odessa?"

"Well, not exactly, except that it is also in the Crimean peninsula. It is a much smaller port than Odessa."

"What is it, old boy?"

"Gold, Mary—solid bullion to the tune of something like four

7

hundred thousand sterling."

"How on earth does it come there? It doesn't seem like the Soviet Government to leave bullion to that amount lying round loose."

Rymer chuckled. Mary's quickness of perception was an eternal joy to the adventurer.

"Nor would they if they knew where to lay their hands on it. But they do know it is in Odjiska, and that is where the rub comes. But I'll tell you what Halloran told me."

Forthwith he began and related the tale which he had heard from the shipchandler. Mary listened in silence, but her quick mind was following every point, and when he had finished she nodded her little head thoughtfully.

"You are right—it is not going to be easy. It will take some thinking out, this problem. What terms does Halloran offer?"

"The usual—a quarter, and he stands all expenses, which means an unlimited drawing account."

"It is worth half on a risky game such as this is bound to be."

"I know, my dear; but what can we do? Unfortunately, Halloran holds the trump cards, and even if we could finance it ourselves I would not double-cross him. He is too useful. Besides, a hundred thousand in bullion is a pretty nice haul."

Mary did not answer until they entered the shade of the palm-grove, and Rymer had made a tour of the place to make sure that no natives were lurking about the place. But when he rejoined her she said:

"You couldn't take the share in bullion. It would he too difficult to get rid of. Bullion isn't like anything else. It isn't bought and sold like merchandise."

"Of course not. But that end of it would be Halloran's job. I should arrange that he was to hand us our share on the form of a draft. He will play square, Mary. I am just as useful to him as he is to me. Otherwise he wouldn't have cabled to London for me. There are dozens of men kicking about the Mediterranean who would jump at a chance like this."

"But none of them could handle it like you." she returned softly.

Rymer patted her shoulder. They were a strange pair, those two—the big, bearded adventurer and the slip of a girl, who, for all that, had a wonderful nerve and a courage that equalled the man's. And Rymer would have been the first to confess that nine times out of ten it was her quick mind which saw a solution almost instantly where he would have needed hours or days to thrash out the problem.

"I'd have been stumped again and again if it hadn't been for you, my dear," he said quietly. "And I am hanged if I can see a way out of this business. I'll bet two-thirds of the population of Odjiska are looking for that gold, every one of them a Soviet agent. And how the deuce we are to lift it under their noses I can't see for the life of me."

The girl turned and gazed dreamily back towards the slender minarets of the mosque which stood up startlingly clear against the blue of the late afternoon sky.

Beyond those minarets was the Mediterranean, and north, in almost a direct line as she was gazing, the Dardanelles and the Bosphorus, the Golden Horn and the Black Sea. And there under the sinister wing of the Soviet, was the prize of which Halloran had heard, had scented out like some yellow-polled carrion bird.

Gold! Yellow Gold!

There is nothing like it in the world to rouse the passions and greed of man. Diamonds, emeralds, pearls, rubies—soul-stealing are they; but gold—there is something about the gleam of raw yellow metal that goes deeper than anything else, and it was of this Mary Trent was thinking as she gazed dreamily towards the north.

"Did Halloran say in what form the bullion is?" she asked suddenly.

"Ingots or bricks—he didn't know for sure."

"They would both be the same to handle?"

"Yes."

Again she was silent for a few moments, then:

"It would be practically impossible for us to get into that part of Russia by any overland route, wouldn't it?"

"It could be done, but it would take a long time. We should have to travel by a very roundabout way; either get into Russia from Central Europe or by the north and then by rail down to the Crimea."

"But not so difficult by sea?"

"Not if our identity was not discovered."

"But surely Halloran can fix up papers for us."

"I should think so. He says he can handle all the outside details— that is, after we reach Odjiska, we must handle the thing on our own."

"Then it would have to be by sea. And after that would come the main problem of getting the gold away. We could never do it, old boy, unless we had a ship of our own."

"No. I have thought of that. But it is a bit of a stickler."

"Wait a minute. If Halloran will finance everything as he says, then, in his business it ought to be easy enough for him to get hold of some sort of craft that would serve the purpose. We should have to appear at Odjiska just like any other cargo boat, and that means cargo, a genuine shipment."

"We could run up in ballast if we could get a cargo there," remarked Rymer thoughtfully. "That is a good suggestion of yours, Mary. I'll mull it over. I don't know how difficult it would be to pick up a load of some sort at Odjiska, but Halloran ought to know about that. The chief shipments from Crimean ports in the old days consisted of wheat, but, with the Russian crops as short as they have been since the Soviet took the saddle I don't, know. It is worth inquiring into. But that doesn't get us the gold."

"It is a start, at any rate," she rejoined, smiling up at him. "If we can achieve that first step, then we can give our minds to the second. Once we get to Odjiska, the next thing is to locate the gold, and then—"

"Which means that you approve of the affair," put in Rymer.

She nodded her head seriously.

"Why not? That is, if I go along, too. Funds are running low with us, and there is something about the idea of taking away this gold from under the noses of the Bolshevists that appeals to me. When are you seeing Halloran?"

"To-morrow morning."

"Well, why not make that suggestion to him and see what he says?"

Rymer squeezed her arm.

"I will, little one, I will. And now let us stroll back. There are some fellaheen coming this way, and the muezzin will be calling soon."

So, nestling in against his arm contentedly, Mary allowed him to guide her out of the grove and across the naked sand towards the distant minarets.

It was just half-past eleven when Rymer walked into the shipchandler's shop the following morning. He found Halloran in the back room, bent, as usual, over his desk, and as soon as the big man had seated himself, the other simply gave vent to one word of inquiry.

"Well?"

"I've been thinking things over and discussing them with my partner," responded Rymer. "I take it you knew she was with me."

"Of course. What decision have you arrived at?"

"I am inclined to take it on, providing you can overcome certain difficulties at this end."

"What are they?"

Briefly Rymer explained the idea which had been suggested by Mary Trent.

"I hold master's papers, as you know." he went on. "But the chief difficulty is the boat and the cargo at Odjiska."

Halloran spat a great stream of tobacco juice into a box of sand.

"Cargo at Odjiska! What about a cargo to Odjiska, and come away in ballast? My information is that the bullion is in lump bricks or ingots, it doesn't matter which— but, I know, further, that they are painted black to give the appearance of ordinary pig-iron. If you took a cargo of cotton or wheat up to Odjiska—the Bolshies are more anxious to buy wheat than they are to export it—you could come out in ballast; and if you do find that bullion, why couldn't you chuck it in among the ballast?"

"There might be something in that suggestion, but you said the Soviet agents were fine-tooth combing every ship that entered and left. It would be a risk to have the bullion among the ballast. If the slightest whisper got out, they would examine every lump before they allowed us to clear."

"Well, I've made the suggestion for what it may be worth. If you take a cargo up I can get hold of a small tramp at Alexandria and a load of wheat. I know a man, too, in Odjiska, to whom I can consign the lot, and he might be useful to you when you get there; but watch him. On the other hand, if you think it better to go up in ballast, then it would be unwise to sail from an Egyptian port."

"I think it would be better to go up in ballast. If we did that, what port would you suggest?"

"Marseilles. It's a big port, and you could slide out without anyone thinking anything about it. Going out of an Egyptian port in ballast is different."

"What about a boat at Marseilles?"

"Easy enough. I can fix that by cable in twenty-four hours. I have an agent there who will attend to all the details. Let me know which you decide on, and I'll get busy."

"I think I'll stick to the first idea," remarked Rymer slowly. "My partner's instinct is pretty sound, and I'll ride her suggestion."

"All right," grunted Halloran. "Let's get down to figures."

For the next half-hour they argued back and forth, figuring over charter party, money, stores, crew and whatnot.

At the end of that time they had fixed on a round sum which it was agreed should see Rymer through to Odjiska with a safe margin in hand, and from there he could cable to Halloran how much he would need to cover whatever cargo he decided to bring away, fixing on wheat for the time being, but if that was out of the question, then he would try and pick up a load of rye or barley.

It was decided, further, that Rymer should return to Marseilles by an Orient boat that was due to pass through the Canal that same evening, which meant that Halloran would have a clear five or six days to fix things up by cable with his agent at the French port.

Mary received the decision with her usual nonchalance. She was quite satisfied with whatever details Rymer might arrange once he had given consideration to any suggestions she might have to make. She was a remarkably wise little woman, was Mary Trent, and she knew just when to tighten the curb, and when to leave it slack.

So she was blithe enough that evening when they left the Continental and joined the big homeward-bound Orient boat which swung at anchor out in the harbour until a little after midnight.

It was the policy of the two, when travelling together, to appear as strangers to each other, and for this reason each travelled out to the ship in a separate bumboat. Nor did they speak outwardly again until they were once more ashore at Marseilles, although, to be sure, not a day had passed but that they had communicated with each other in some way.

At Marseilles they betook themselves to a certain small hotel near the old basin where they had stayed often before, and where they did not run the risk they would have met at one of the larger places.

Rymer had given the name of this hotel to Halloran to be transmitted to the latter's agent, and early the evening they landed this agent visited them.

He was a typical Provencal—stout, swarthy, genial of manner, almost childlike at times, but as shrewd in business as a combination of Greek and Jew and Levantine.

Halloran had apparently advised him at some length what was required, for when he had bowed to Rymer, and, after the fashion of his kind, had ogled Mary, he craved permission to be seated, and drew a folded packet of papers from his pocket.

"Monsieur Halloran has told me of your requirements," he said in laboured English, but Rymer quickly assured him that both he and Mary spoke French fluently. So, reverting to his own tongue, the Provencal went on: "I have here particulars of four different ships that might suit your purpose—two are under the French flag, one under the Spanish flag, and the fourth under the Greek flag.

"In size and accommodation the latter ship seems to me to be the most suitable; but I would warn you that the Greek flag is none too popular in the Russian ports of the Black Sea since the Russians have been philandering with the Turks."

Here he paused to ogle Mary again, as if it were his dearest wish that he was a Russian and she Turkish. But his shrewd little eyes were business-like enough when he resumed.

"Yes, monsieur, as I have said, the Greek boat is not too large and is well fitted. One of the French boats is in very poor shape, but the other is in fair order. The Spanish boat is, however, the one, taken all in all, which I should advise you to choose, providing you have one qualification."

"That is?"

"That you can speak Spanish."

"I have lived in Spain and Spanish America at different times for considerable periods. I know the language well. But I would remind you that my master's papers are English."

The Frenchman snapped his fingers airily. "Pouf! That is nothing, monsieur, a mere matter of form. The present captain of the ship is amenable to reason. He is three parts owner, and for a figure one which Monsieur Halloran has authorised me to offer—is willing to retire for the time being and place the ship and crew entirely under your command."

"That sounds all right, monsieur. How large is she?"

"She has, as you would say in English, twelve hundred tons."

"About the right size for this business," muttered Rymer. Then aloud: "I take it that she has complied with the international law and is fitted with wireless?"

"But of course!"

"Officers and crew?"

"There is a first officer and a second; the crew is of the sort one always finds about this sea, monsieur. They number twenty-four not including the engineer and eight men in the stokehold."

"She seems to be pretty well manned for a craft of that size."

"She has been employed off the coast of Morocco, monsieur, where things are a little difficult at present."

Rymer understood what that meant. He needed to hear no more, to know that despite the ostensible Spanish nationality of the captain, he had probably been running arms to the Riffs under the French and Spanish blockade.

"Is she all ready to put to sea?"

"Not at once but in, say, ten days. The Greek boat could be got away in three days."

"I am anxious to lose no time but, on the other hand, if the Greek flag is not popular in the Russian ports, then more might be lost than gained."

"That is exactly as I calculate, monsieur. I do not know the nature of the cargo you go to bring, but Monsieur Halloran advises me that it is of an important nature. If I might suggest that you look over the Greek and the Spaniard to-morrow and then decide? If neither suits we can then inspect the two French ships."

"I think that would be the best plan, monsieur. At what time?"

"At whatever hour you will, monsieur."

"Shall we say at ten o'clock? At my office?"

"That will suit."

With that the Frenchman drew out a card which he handed to Rymer. He had already introduced himself as Monsieur Bompard, and Rymer saw that the address of the office was no great distance from where he and Mary were staying. He saw him out, then he returned to the little private sitting-room where Mary was waiting.

"Well, little one," he remarked as he lit a cigar, "what do you think?"

Mary puckered her brow.

"It sounds all right," she returned, slowly, "and because he is Halloran's agent I suppose it must be all right. But just the same, I don't like the man!"

Rymer laughed.

"Woman's instinct again, eh? The type is not a usual one to you,

Mary, that is all. Bompard is all right. Besides, as Halloran's agent, he daren't be anything else. Halloran has a long arm and, incidentally, so have I."

"It isn't that. But I feel as if that man Bompard would do anything for money."

"Well, most of us are like that."

"How much is Halloran paying him for his services?"

"The usual commission for such business, I suppose. That would be so much percentage of the charter party money."

The girl looked thoughtful as she lit a cigarette, then:

"Supposing, just for the sake of argument, this man Bompard got to know the nature of the cargo we are going after—got to learn its value—wouldn't the ordinary charter party commission seem pretty small to him?"

"Well, he doesn't know, and we are not likely to tell him. Anyway, all that part of the business is Halloran's affair. My end of it doesn't begin until I get my feet on the bridge of the ship and get her to sea."

Still Mary did not let the matter rest.

"Don't forget, old boy, that the people who got that bullion down as far as Odjiska are not going to leave it there without moving heaven and earth to get it out of Russia. What has become of them?"

"You can search me, dear girl," he responded slangily. "Halloran didn't know. I take it, it is as you say, that they are trying to figure out some scheme for getting it away. That is why I might be almost tempted to settle on the Greek ship instead of the other. Time is the chief essence of this business, that is until we get to Odjiska."

"Supposing they should make Marseilles their base? It might seem a good deal of a coincidence, but then we picked it above all other ports in the Mediterranean and they might do the same."

Rymer did not answer at once. He poured himself a brandy and soda, and smoked in silence while he sipped half the contents. Then he set the glass down and seated himself on the couch beside her.

"Not getting cold feet are you, Mary?" he asked quietly.

"Of course not. I am as keen as you to put this affair through. But in the past so many coups have failed with us over little things that, this time, it is such a big thing, I don't want there to be any hitch. If we could pull this off think what it would mean to us, dear man! It would make it possible for us to live in peace and comfort!"

Rymer laid his hand on hers.

"Getting tired of the game, my dear?"

She flashed a quick look at him, then laid her cheek against his sleeve while his free arm went round her shoulder.

"Not tired of anything when I am with you," she whispered, "but—but there are times when I want so for us to have peace; where we can live quietly without fear, just away from everything at Abbey Towers."

His fingers tightened over hers and he stroked her soft hair.

"I could never give up the game entirely, little one," he answered. "If I said I would, I should be lying. But I promise you, if we pull this thing off I'll go to Abbey Towers and we'll rusticate there just as long as you wish. You shall do everything there is in your heart to do."

A hot tear struck the back of his hand and he laid the cigar aside. Then he took her in his arms and petted her as he would a child. Whatever he may have been in the realm of crime, Huxton Rymer had nothing but tenderness for Mary Trent, and he had held her heart for a long time.

But half an hour later Rymer reverted to what the girl had been saying.

"I'm not saying your instinct is right, about Bompard, and I'm not saying it is wrong, my dear. It wouldn't be such a coincidence as you seem to think for anyone else who was after that bullion to choose Marseilles as a base of operations. There isn't a more suitable spot in the Mediterranean. But even if those others did run across Bompard he wouldn't dare double-cross us. Halloran holds him too hard."

"That man would sell his own mother for money, if it was enough," she said vehemently. "I don't like him and I don't trust him. Don't forget that there is enough gold there to tempt almost anyone, and a man like Bompard could be bought with a very small portion of it."

"But he wouldn't dare, little one, he wouldn't dare. However, I shall keep my eyes open, and at the first sign of anything I shall know what to do."

In thinking that Bompard would not dare double-cross them, however, Rymer was wrong, as events in the near future were to show. They left it at that, and after some further discussion of the matter, Mary retired, while Rymer went for a short walk along by the

16

old basin before turning in.

CHAPTER 3. Sexton Blake is Told a Strange Story—An Unexpected Tragedy.

WHILE Huxton Rymer and Mary Trent were engaged in Marseilles with the first part of their campaign, it would be as well to revert to certain events which took place in London some ten days before Rymer received his first code message from Halloran.

On a warm sunny morning in August, Sexton Blake, the famous criminologist, and his youthful assistant, Tinker, were seated at work in the consulting-room at Baker Street when Mrs. Bardell, the house keeper, knocked at the door and entered, bearing a card upon a tray.

A glance at the name showed Blake that his visitor was none other than Brigadier General Cotter, a gentleman whom he had met on one or two occasions and who had been, he knew, attached at one time to the Kerensky forces in Russia as a liaison officer.

He instructed Mrs. Bardell to show the visitor in, and a few moments later the general, a tall, upright man whose iron-grey moustache indicated early middle age, entered accompanied by a second gentleman of somewhat foreign appearance.

When Blake had greeted the general, the latter's companion was introduced as Count Torsky, and when Blake had made them comfortable in two easy chairs, the general went on:

"It is on behalf of my friend Count Torsky that I have come to see you, Mr. Blake. I hope you can spare us half an hour or so!"

"With pleasure, General Cotter. Before we go into the object of your visit may I offer you one of these cigars, or perhaps Count Torsky would prefer a cigarette of his own country?"

The general indicated that he would he happy to sample one of Blake's choice Partagas, but his companion elected to smoke one of the rare Russian cigarettes which, to tell the truth, Blake kept chiefly for the benefit of his friend, Mademoiselle Yvonne, who was decidedly partial to them.

With the smoke curling upwards through the wide beam of sunlight that came through the window, the general went on:

"Count Torsky, arrived in London last evening from Paris. When I was liaison officer with General Kerensky's army in Russia I had the pleasure of meeting Count Torsky, and indeed we did considerable campaigning together. He is staying at the Hotel Venetia for the present, and last night he told me in confidence why he had

18

come to London to see me.

"It is a strange tale, Mr. Blake, and one which has a certain element of romance about it. My friend, Count Torsky, begged for my advice, and while I am, of course, willing to do anything in my power to assist him, I am unfortunately bound by the fact that I am still in Government service. But that did not preclude me making a suggestion, which was that we should come and see you, for I believe if any man can find a way out of the—er—predicament in which Count Torsky finds himself you are that man."

Blake bowed his acknowledgment of the compliment.

"Just what is the difficulty?" he asked.

"I will tell you. You know Russia, of course, Mr. Blake?"

"Parts of it intimately—most of it to a certain extent."

"Have you ever been at Petrovad?"

"Yes, two or three times."

"Then you will remember the big domed church there."

"Naturally. I found it most interesting. If I recollect rightly the large dome as well as the two smaller ones are covered with pure gold plates. I was told the approximate amount of gold, but the figure escapes me for the moment."

"That is right. The value has been placed variously from two hundred thousand pounds sterling to a quarter of a million. Well, Mr. Blake, the gold that was on those domes as well as the treasure which was in the church have inspired this visit to you. I will be more clear.

"The church—one of the orthodox Russian Greek churches—is, or was, part of the personal estate entail of the Grand Duke Boris, who was killed in the revolution. His heir was the Grand Duke Nicholas, who is at present living in retirement just outside Paris, and it is he, therefore, who is the rightful owner of the church and town of Petrovad, together with several thousand *versts* of land surrounding the place."

"Which means also the gold plates on the domes of the church," put in Blake.

"Exactly. The Soviet Government have been so busy in the west and south and through the Caspians that for some time Petrovad, which is in a very isolated region as you know, escaped their attention, or, I should say, the attention of the central Moscow Soviet. Of course, in common with other parts, a local Soviet was established at Petrovad, but the people there are only half-hearted Bolshevists, and of a very devout turn of mind, with the result that no attempt was made to strip the church such as had been done in other parts.

"Count Torsky, who is a follower of the Grand Duke Nicholas, conceived the idea, of making his way back into Russia—he had escaped some months before the time of which I speak—and trying to bring out the gold plates on the domes of the church at Petrovad, as well as the golden altar treasure, and so on. He did not tell the grand duke what his intentions were. He simply asked for some months' leave of absence, which was readily granted, and together with several other Royalist patriots, returned to Russia in disguise.

"It is not necessary for me to go into detail as to their subsequent movements after crossing the frontier, but it is sufficient to say that out of five who started three, including my friend, Count Torsky, succeeded in eluding the Soviet Cheka, and got through to Petrovad.

"For some weeks they worked quietly there, hidden by Royalist sympathisers, and, after pulling every possible string and employing every form of persuasion, they finally achieved their purpose, which was nothing less than to strip the gold plates from the domes of the church and to melt them down with the gold altar ornaments into bullion. It was a great feat to pull it off under the very noses of the Soviet."

Blake shot a glance of respect at the young Russian. It didn't need any elaboration for him to realise just what a feat it must have been.

To get into Russia was difficult enough for men who carried their lives in their hands from the moment they crossed the frontier; to travel hundreds of miles through the Soviet stronghold, where every man was an agent of the dreaded Cheka was an even greater thing; but to lurk for weeks in one place, and finally to bring off such a coup as General Cotter had just related needed more than just nerve—it needed sheer, blind patriotism that counted, life itself as nothing.

"I can appreciate that it indeed was a feat, general," he said quietly.

"A man who has led your sort of life would," responded the other. "Well, to continue. These young men not only succeeded in melting down all the gold— actually some two tons of the metal— into bricks which they painted black to give the appearance of ordinary pig iron, but they got clean away from Petrovad with it, and, despite the Soviet, landed it safely at Odjiska, in the Crimea—a journey of some three weeks' duration by slow caravan. In the meantime the affair was reported to Moscow, and a regiment appeared at Petrovad with the usual result. The members of the local Soviet were executed, and more than a hundred of the inhabitants massacred. But that did not get back the gold.

"On the other hand, the Cheka seemed to realise that the loot had been taken in the direction of the Crimea, for by the time the little caravan reached Odjiska the whole peninsula was swarming with Soviet agents. Count Torsky and his companions knew that it would be hopeless then to try and get the bullion out of the country. Every craft that entered or left at every port on the Black Sea, no matter how small, was subjected to the most rigid scrutiny, and indeed, it was as much as they could manage to get out of the country with a whole skin.

"That was something over a month ago, and for some time past Count Torsky and his two companions have been busy at Constantinople, at Athens, at Naples, at Barcelona and at Marseilles trying to devise some scheme to get the gold away from Odjiska, but without success. Then came tragedy. At Marseilles Count Torsky's two companions were murdered. In some way the cheka agents must have learned of their participation in the affair, and their appointed assassins succeeded in tracking them to Marseilles. Count Torsky escaped, and, realising that he could do nothing alone, made his way to Paris.

"He could not take up the matter with the Grand Duke Nicholas, who, of course, knew nothing of what had been going on, and could only recognise a fait accompli, since he is living as the guest of France. Therefore, Count Torsky decided to come across to London and ask my advice. The result is this visit to you. Now, sir, you have solved a good many tough problems and have cracked a good many tough nuts. Can you crack this one? I believe, if you will set your mind to it, you can do so."

Blake puffed thoughtfully for some moments before replying. He needed no telling just what a tough nut it was, but at that moment he was not thinking of that, nor, indeed, of the problem proper. His mind was dwelling on the two murders which had taken place in Marseilles—dwelling on those two young men who had gone down under the treacherous knives of the Cheka.

Suddenly he looked at Count Torsky. "The bullion—is it hidden in Odjiska or near there?"

"In the town." was the reply, in perfect English. "I have brought with me, sir, all the documents connected with the matter. The originals are in Russian, but I can give you copies in French or English."

"If you care to trust me with the originals it will be all the same," responded Blake, with a smile. "I have a fair knowledge of your language."

"Certainly, sir. I did not know you were acquainted with the Russian."

"I can go into those later. But perhaps you will give me a few brief details as to where the gold is hidden, and so on."

"With pleasure. As my friend, General Cotter, has told you, we succeeded in reaching Odjiska, but to attempt to get the gold away by sea was hopeless at that time. The whole peninsula was alive with the agents of the Cheka. My two companions—poor, unfortunate fellows—and myself managed to steal a small boat and leave the coast. We look a keg of water and a little food, and after some days were picked up in the Black Sea by a Greek ship, which gave us passage to Constantinople. General Cotter has given you a brief history of our movements since that time, ending with the murder of my two companions at Marseilles."

"Is the gold hidden in some haphazard place which you selected, or is it in the care of some reliable person?"

"It is in the care of a most reliable man— a Royalist to the heart. He is a ship-chandler and blacksmith in a small way in Odjiska, but before the last revolution he was a prosperous merchant at Petrovad, and a tenant of the Grand Duke Boris. He will guard the secret with his life."

"But if the place is full of Cheka spies then discovery may come at any moment," remarked Blake,

"That is true, but it is a risk which had to be taken."

"Quite so. How is the gold hidden?"

"That even I cannot tell you. I do not know. We agreed that it was safer that only one person should know—the one who guards it."

"Um. You say you were at various ports in the Mediterranean trying to devise some plan for getting the gold away. Wasn't that rather risky if the Cheka agents were on your trail?"

"We worked with great caution through the local loyalist Russian organisations. But I agree with you, sir, that it was risky. In some way there must have been a leakage, as witness the murder of my two companions."

"Did the French police succeed in discovering anything?"

"Nothing at all. They were murdered on the waterfront and their bodies thrown into the harbour. But each body bore the secret mark of the Cheka, so there is no doubt that agents of that organisation killed them. (The Cheka is the Soviet secret service organisation whose powers are greater and whose doings are far more terrible than the Spanish Inquisition of old.—Ed.)

"What plan were you following?"

"We explored several, but that which seemed the most feasible was the one we were employed on in Marseilles. It was our idea to proceed to Odjiska with a ship—either in disguise or to send a boat under some trustworthy person. There are many of the former naval officers of the Tsarist navy living as refugees in France, and we counted on getting the assistance of some of them as officers and crew. But before anything definite had been decided upon, the double murder brought things to a stop."

Blake looked thoughtful.

"The idea strikes me as being about the only method that could be employed," he said at last. "Odjiska is a seaport, and from what you have told me it would be out of the question to try and transport the gold by land. Besides, even if it could be got away from Odjiska there would be hundreds if not thousands of miles to cover before coming to the frontier."

"Exactly so, sir,"

"Even if the Cheka agents suspect the gold to be hidden in Odjiska, I take it they have planted their spies at every spot along the Russian seafront of the Black Sea."

"Yes—as I said, and more particularly in Crimean ports. Odessa is full of them at all times, and I know from certain information that thousands of extra spies have been sent to the south."

"And after reaching Odjiska—what then?"

The Russian spread out his hands in a truly foreign gesture.

"What then, sir! We had no definite plan. We hoped to find a solution when we got there."

"It is a very large quantity of gold, Count. I suppose you have considered the possibility of others besides the Soviet agents trying to get hold of it if they suspect its existence."

"Yes, but how can they learn of it? Every man who was in the thing was to be trusted completely."

"Do you mean you can count on every soul who came with the caravan from Petrovad?"

"They were loyal, I am sure."

But Blake shook his head.

"Gold is like nothing else on earth, Count, It is uncanny the way its presence makes itself known. It is as if the dead metal were not dead but endowed with life. Once, in India, I remember killing a rat in the club chambers where I was staying at the time. I took the vermin by the tail and walked from the chambers to the beach, which was close at hand. Before throwing it away, I looked up into the sky in every possible direction. Not a single thing was there to fleck the blue when I cast the rat across the sand.

"Still I stood looking up and then, some ten minutes later, I saw, high, high up, a tiny speck which grew more and more distinct as it approached. It was a kite— one of the great scavenging hawks of India. I am quite sure that when I first stepped on to the beach that kite was many, many miles away—too far for sight and too far for scent. And yet it sensed that dead rat and came straight as an arrow to the spot. It is the same with gold—I don't know how or why. No man can explain it, but it is so."

The Slavic mind of the Russian was stirred at Blake's words, and he shifted uneasily as he said:

"It is so, I believe, sir. But how could anyone know of this gold."

Blake shrugged.

"I merely make the suggestion. It is a contingency to be guarded against. If it has leaked out then you may take it as certain that others will be after it, and those who follow such trails indulge in desperate ways."

"But, sir, will you give me your aid? Can I hope that you will assist me in this? It means much and, sir, I am authorised to tell you that whether you succeed or fail you may name your own fee. I have discussed this phase with my friend, General Cotter, and he has suggested that it might be best to name a definite fee for your work and time even if failure attends your efforts; and a percentage basis on the value of the gold in case of success."

"I am not prepared yet to say whether I will take the case or not,

Count. I acknowledge that there are certain features of it which appeal to me strongly; and it would seem a great pity if that gold fell into the hands of the Cheka or some gang of adventurers, after all the dangers you and your companions have been through.

"But before saying 'yes' or 'no', I should like the opportunity to read the documents which you have brought and to get a detailed grasp of the whole business. If you are willing to give me time to do that, I shall then let you have a definite answer —say by tomorrow morning."

"Certainly, sir, with all my heart, I shall eagerly await your advices."

Blake locked the envelope containing the documents in his desk and then, after few more minutes conversation, General Cotter and Count Torsky took their departure, Blake promising to communicate with the Russian at his hotel by ten o'clock the following morning.

When they were gone, he re-seated himself at his desk and was about to settle down again to the work on which he had been engaged when Tinker, who had been a close listener to all that had gone before, said:

"I say, guv'nor, it would be a bit of a lark to have a shot at that gold, wouldn't it?"

Blake grunted.

"More of a lark than you think, perhaps. If you are looking for that kind of excitement, you had better go out to the Zoo and get the keeper to allow you to go into the tiger's cage and twist his tail."

"But two tons of the real stuff, sir! Gee! I'd like to see what it looks like when it is piled up in one heap. Aren't you going to read those papers now?"

Blake frowned.

"Get on with your work," he snapped. "We will go into them this evening."

And with that Tinker had to be content.

But that evening Blake took the bundle of documents from his desk and, with a Russian dictionary beside him to refresh his memory, set to work, with Tinker at his elbow, to jot down shorthand notes of anything Blake might have to say as he went along. For the better part of two hours the pair worked industriously, and then, with something of a sigh of relief, Blake pushed the last paper away from him.

"A fine bit of work, my lad," he remarked as he stuffed, his pipe.

"Any Britisher might be proud of that job. This young man, Count Torsky, had his nerve with him all right. If one wrote out the thing as a magazine yarn it would be called far-fetched."

"Like some of your cases which are written up at times, guv'nor."

"Quite so. But the point is that something like four hundred thousand pounds sterling in gold bullion is lying bidden at the port of Odjiska in the Crimea and only one individual knows, or did know, its exact location. From what Count Torsky said, and also from the details in these papers, it seems that this person is a sort of shipchandler and blacksmith combined. There is a quaint idea in that, young 'un."

"How so, guv'nor?"

"That a blacksmith should be the sole guardian of the gold treasure from one of the richest churches in Russia. Tsar to blacksmith; blacksmith to Tsar. But after all, Peter the Great was an ordinary shipbuilder."

"And Riza Khan, the new Shah of Persia, was just a common soldier," added Tinker.

"Quite so, my lad. I am glad to see that you keep abreast of current events. But to return to this gold. If it is still safe then it is in the care of one, Petrov, who, according to Count Torsky, will guard it with his life. If the Cheka agents or any others who may be after the gold are still ignorant of that, then we are so far one step ahead of them. But on the other hand it lies in a Soviet stronghold, surrounded by thousands of Soviet spies whose chief aim in life is to kill. To lift the gold from under their noses, to get it clean away, appears to me to be almost an insoluble problem. It is going to take some doing, young 'un, some doing."

"That means you are going to tackle it," burst out Tinker. "I always know when you talk that way your mind is made up."

"Don't be too sure young 'un. And now be quiet! I want to think."

Forthwith Blake dropped into one of the low, saddle-bag chairs, and with his pipe gripped between his teeth, half-closed his eyes.

Tinker returned to his desk, but at the end of half an hour when Blake showed no signs of stirring, he picked up his cap and stole out softly for his work was finished and the soft August evening was too fine to stick indoors when Blake was in one of his thinking fits.

Ten o'clock found him back, but still Blake sat as if he hadn't once moved all the time the lad was out. Tinker would have thought so but for the fact that he could see the pipe had been refilled. He was on the point of going along to his own room when Blake opened his eyes, and in a dreamy voice said:

"Do you remember reading how the silkworm was first brought to Europe, Tinker?"

Tinker scratched his head. He knew he had read of that incident and knew it had taken place somewhere about the fourteenth or fifteenth century; but at that moment he could not recall just how it had been done.

"Look it up and impress it upon your mind, young 'un. I'll tell you now but read it afterwards for yourself. It was this way. In the fifteenth century the silkworm was known only in China and the penalty for taking even one cocoon out of the country was death. After Vasco do Gama sailed to the Indies and up the China coast the Portuguese priests followed in his track, just as the Spanish priests followed Columbus and Cortez and all the other Spanish conquistadores to the New World. Well, there were two priests who got into China, and they soon realised what a big prize it would be if they could take some silk cocoons back to Portugal. They set their wits to work and after some time hit on a plan which they thought might work. They put it into effect, and when they finally succeeded in getting out of the country they carried as walking-staves two long bits of bamboo. And in a hollow section of each bamboo was a silkworm cocoon."

"I remember now, guv'nor, of course. But what about that?"

Blake rose, and with a yawn knocked the ashes from his pipe.

"Just this, my lad. If we are to get that bullion out of Odjiska we have got to be as subtle as those two Portuguese priests. Unless we can hit on some plan that is equally simple, there isn't a chance. It must be so simple and so obvious that it will fool the closest observer—even more subtle than the idea of the 'Purloined Letter.' And I have the germ of an idea— just the germ, of one!"

"My hat, guv'nor, what is it?"

"Not yet, young 'un; not even to you."

Tinker was about to speak again when the telephone rang shrilly and Blake, who was nearest the desk, picked up the receiver.

"Yes. Oh, yes, General Cotter," Tinker heard him say; then,

"what—incredible— yes, yes—I shall come there at once, general; within a quarter of an hour." With that he hung up the receiver and swung sharply.

"Get round to the garage and get the Grey Panther," he ordered. "Count Torsky has been found dead in his room at the Venetia!"

Tinker gaped once at the startling news, then he fled.

CHAPTER 4.   A Ghastly Affair—The End of Count Torsky— The Result of Blake's Investigations.

ON arriving at the Venetia, where he was so well known, there was no need for Blake to inquire which way he should go. As soon as he entered the lobby, the reception-clerk signalled to him, and when Blake bent over the desk said, in a low tone:

"General Cotter is waiting for you, sir. Mr. Browning,"—the manager of the Venetia— "is with him, and we expect an inspector from Scotland Yard at any moment. Will you please go up? The suite is number twenty-three on the second floor."

Blake nodded, and beckoned to Tinker. They ascended in the lift to the second floor and Blake, who knew the great caravanserai from cellar to roof, needed no guide to show him to number twenty-three.

He strode along the corridor to the right, and after passing a few closed doors came to the one he sought. He tapped on it lightly and a low voice called, 'enter.' Blake turned the handle and he and Tinker stepped into one of the luxurious sitting-rooms for which the Venetia is famous.

Seated in an easy chair with a very grave expression on his face was General Colter. He jumped to his feet on seeing the pair from Baker Street.

"Thank heaven you have come, Blake. I thought it was the inspector from the Yard. I did not think you could got here so soon."

"I came at once, general. What a terrible affair! Where is—"

The general pointed to a closed door on the right.

"We have laid him on his bed. The hotel doctor is with him now, also the hotel manager. It is indeed a terrible affair."

"But how did it happen? How much do you know?"

"Very little. I had an appointment at the War Office this evening which I could not break—some details of army estimates. But I promised Count Torsky I would call in here on my way home and spend an hour with him. He had left word in the office that when I arrived I was to be shown up at once. It was just after ten when I got here. A page brought me up, and when, after knocking several times there was no answer, I turned the handle and entered.

"The moment I stepped over the threshold I saw poor Torsky lying face down on the carpet, his head towards the door. From the position of the chair at the desk, and the condition of the papers on it, it was obvious he had been writing while waiting for me. Indeed, there is a half-finished letter there now.

"I turned him over and soon saw that he had been shot through the heart. I lost several minutes in choking off the page, who began to whimper, and then I telephoned down to the office and asked the manager to come up. I know it is better in such cases to leave the body as one finds it, but it was difficult for the doctor to make the examination on the floor, so I told them to carry it in and lay it on the bed."

Blake walked to the desk and then, turning, took a few steps in the direction of the door. All of a sudden he flopped flat on his face, while the general and Tinker looked puzzled. But Blake was on his feet again in a moment, and with a glance of inquiry at General Cotter asked: "Was he in about that position?"

"Yes; almost exactly."

"Wait a moment, please. Will you sit down at the desk, general. I want to test out something before the man from the Yard arrives. That is right. Now I am going to step into the hall for a moment. When I knock I want you to call to me to enter. As I do so, I want you to rise and start to walk towards me. Do you follow?"

"Yes."

Blake stepped into the corridor and closed the door. He waited only a moment before knocking. At the sound of the general's voice he opened the door and started towards the centre of the room. As he did so the general got up and walked in his direction. Then Blake paused and nodded.

"Before I hear anything more I am willing to wager that some time before you reached the hotel Count Torsky had another visitor. Quite recently I had a case the conditions of which were almost exactly similar to this. You will recall the affair at Brighton, Tinker!"

"Why yes, sir! The victim of that was in just that position."

"Quite so. It is only a snap theory, general. But I think we shall do well to lose no time in finding out if someone did visit him. But first, I should like to hear what the doctor has to say."

At that moment the bedroom door opened and the hotel doctor and Browning came out. They greeted Blake, and then in answer to Blake's question the doctor said:

"I should say he was alive at nine o'clock, Mr. Blake. He met his death sometime after that hour. Rigor mortis is not yet fully pronounced."

Blake turned to the manager.

"Browning, would you please make inquiries at the reception desk and find out if anyone asked for Count Torsky between nine and ten—before General Cotter called?"

"Certainly, at once!"

With that the manager went to the telephone which stood on the escritoire, and, lifting the receiver asked to be put through to the reception office.

In the meantime Blake entered the bedroom, and, pulling down the sheet which covered the still form, made a brief examination. As the doctor had left the clothing of the upper part of the body open, it was plain to be seen that General Cotter had been right. There was a small hole just over the heart. Blake drew up the sheet and returned to the other room. Browning was just hanging up the receiver, and as Blake entered he said:

"Yes, there was a visitor about twenty minutes past nine."

"Ah! Did he give a name?"

"He did. It was a foreign name which the reception clerk is finding it difficult to remember. At any rate, he says that the man was a swarthy-looking foreigner, though well dressed. He asked for Count Torsky, and gave his name—the one which the clerk cannot remember. But he recalls that it was only a single name. He telephoned up to Count Torsky and informed him that a visitor had called. Then, on the count's request, he gave the name which had been given him. Count Torsky told him to send the visitor up, which he did. He does not remember having seen the man go out again."

Blake turned to the doctor.

"Have you discovered if the bullet is still in the body, doctor?"

"It must be, if we assume that it was a bullet, which seems certain. There is the puncture of entry, but no mark of exit."

"Did you notice two small scratches on, the left cheek?" went on Blake.

"Yes. I fancy he must have received those in some way when he fell."

Blake made no reply, but striding to the escritoire took off the telephone receiver. He got put through to the reception office, and when he heard the clerk's voice at the other end of the wire he said:

"Mr. Browning has just been speaking with you."

"Yes, sir. Who are you, please?"

"This is Mr. Sexton Blake. I am upstairs with Mr. Browning."

"Oh! Yes, Mr. Blake?"

"Mr. Browning was asking you about a visitor who called to see Count Torsky."

"Yes, sir."

"Now I want you to think carefully, please. You said he gave a name which you could not recall."

"Yes, sir," came the answer a little nervously.

"But you have told Mr. Browning that you are sure it was just a single name and not a double one like so many foreign appellations."

"Yes, sir; I am sure of that."

"All right. Now, listen carefully. Did it, sound anything like this?—Odjiska—Odjiska—O-d-j-i-s-k-a!" And Blake spelled, it out.

There was a startled exclamation at the other end of the wire, and then came the clerk's excited tones:

"Yes, sir! Yes, sir! That was the name. I am perfectly certain now. It has all come back to me."

"Very well. That is all, but you are to keep that to yourself."

"Of course, sir."

With that, Blake hung up the receiver, and as he turned round gave a quick, warning glance at General Cotter, who was gaping at him in frank amazement. How Blake had hit on that he couldn't imagine. But, he was to learn a little later.

Blake had no time to speak further, for just then there came a rap at the door, and Detective-Inspector Thomas of Scotland Yard entered. He looked deliberately round the room, nodding at Blake, Tinker, Browning, and the doctor, then his eyes fell on General Cotter, and, as he recognised that important War Office official, he came quickly to the salute.

Then he waited, as if he expected the general to enlighten him as to what had happened. But General Cotter made a gesture in Blake's direction.

"Ask Mr. Blake, inspector. He can tell you better than anyone else."

Briefly Blake explained to his old friend, Inspector Thomas, that the suite in which they were now gathered had been occupied for the past day or so by Count Torsky, a Russian Royalist refugee and personal friend of General Cotter's. He gave a sketch of the events of the evening as he knew them, although he did not air the theory which he had described to the general. Nor did he say anything about his own conversation with the reception clerk.

"The body is on the bed in the next room," he wound up. "I think Dr. Fraser had better deal with the rest of it."

"I'll have a look at it," was the only remark the inspector made.

The doctor led the way, and with an excuse that he would be back presently, Browning left the room. As soon as the door was closed, General Cotter turned to Blake.

"What is it, Blake? What have you discovered? And what suggested Odjiska to you?"

Blake laid a warning finger on his lips. "I'll explain later. Let us see first what the inspector has to say."

Inspector Thomas and the doctor came out presently, and the man from Scotland Yard looked inquiringly at Blake.

"The doctor tells me you have already made some investigations, Blake. What have you discovered?"

"Very little, I am afraid, Thomas. But I will tell you what I know if you wish."

"Well, I don't know what you are doing on the case, but—"

"Mr. Blake came at my personal request," broke in General Cotter coldly but very distinctly.

"Yes, sir—yes, sir; quite so, sir. Er—he was shot, Blake. I take it you agree?"

"Perfectly, inspector. I think that will be shown at the inquest."

"What about the person who called some time after nine? The doctor says there was a visitor who was shown up."

"That appears to be so. And in my opinion, inspector, when you lay your hands on that man you will have the murderer."

"The murdered man was a Russian, I understand. Do you think it was some sort of a political crime?"

"I do, in a way. When General Cotter entered the room the body was lying like this."

With that, Blake once more assumed a prone position on the floor; then he sprang to his feet. The inspector was watching him closely, but all the time he was thinking that General Cotter needn't have been so officious in having the body removed. And in that the good inspector was quite right.

"As I make it," went on Blake, "Count Torsky was writing at his desk when he was informed over the telephone that someone had called to see him. He asked the name, and if you will inquire of the reception clerk you will find that it was given as 'Odjiska,' which is undoubtedly Russian."

Inspector Thomas immediately made a note of this, asking Blake to spell it. Blake obliged, but did not add that it was the name of a town in the Crimea.

"My opinion is that, as his visitor entered the room, Count Torsky saw that it was not the person he had expected, and rose to his feet. The other immediately drew his weapon and shot, killing the count instantly. Your investigations may lead you to a different conclusion; but you may take that as my theory for what it may be worth."

"Had you met Count What's-his-name before?" asked Thomas quickly.

"Yes. General Cotter brought him to see me on private business this morning."

"Would that business have anything to do with this murder?"

"I can't answer that question, inspector. Even if I could it would not throw any light on your investigations."

"Well, it might," grumbled the other.

"Do you mind if I make a suggestion?" went on Blake, as Thomas stood gazing vaguely about him.

"Anything you like."

"Have you examined the clothes which the dead man was wearing?"

"No—that is, not yet."

"I suggest that you search them. I noticed they were hanging on the back of a chair in the bedroom. Also it might he worth while making an examination of his luggage. You might find some clue as to the motive."

"Have you done so?"

"No."

The inspector turned abruptly and disappeared into the bedroom. The general muttered something about "bumptious ass," but Blake was standing in a listening attitude, and he was not surprised when he heard Thomas calling him. He entered the bedroom, and found Thomas on his knees before a small trunk.

"Take a look at the pockets of that coat, Blake. They are just as I found them."

Blake, who had intended doing exactly what he had suggested to the inspector, picked up the coat and waistcoat, and in a swift examination found that the two lower pockets of the jacket were half inside-out, and that those of the waistcoat were absolutely empty. Even a novice among detectives would have known that the garments had been rifled.

"Now here," grunted Thomas. "The lock of this trunk has been forced, and from the appearance of the interior I should say someone had made a hurried search. Whether they found what they were after or not is another matter."

Blake agreed with the inspector that the contents of the trunk were certainly in a very disordered condition, and extended his scrutiny long enough to assure himself that there wasn't a scrap of paper of any sort in the box.

By this time the inspector had drawn a suit-case from under the bed, and in this instance they saw that the intruder had opened it by the simple process of slitting the leather round the lock.

Like the trunk, the contents were in great confusion, but Blake could find no papers. He was even more interested than the inspector in this discovery, but he did not tell the other why.

The inspector rose.

"I'll put one of my men here for the time being. Better send a plain-clothes constable. Are you going ahead with this case, Blake?"

"Well, I hardly know, Thomas. When General Cotter made the discovery he asked me to come along. I suppose he did so because he had brought the dead man to my house this morning. He is, in a way, the person who will naturally look after the affairs of the unfortunate man, and if he asks my assistance I shall naturally do what I can to help. But he has not done so yet."

"If he does I suppose we can consult together?"

"Of course; we always do when we are on the same case."

"I know. Just the same, I wish the old —I mean, the general hadn't had the body moved."

With that they returned to the sitting-room.

"Inspector Thomas is going to put one of his men in charge, general," he announced. "I suppose you will communicate with the police later."

General Cotter rose.

"Your name is?" he asked, glancing at the inspector.

"Thomas, sir, of the C.I.D."

"Very well, inspector, I shall get through to the commissioner to-morrow, and have a talk with him. In the meantime follow the matter in your own way, but I should advise you to take heed of what Mr. Blake has said. I shall make myself personally responsible for everything connected with the late count's affairs."

"Very good, sir."

"This has been a severe shock to me, Blake," went on the general. "If you have finished here shall we go along together? I should like to have a talk with you."

"Certainly, general." Then to Thomas: "If anything occurs to me, inspector, I shall telephone through to you."

The general, Blake, and Tinker took their departure, leaving Thomas and the doctor behind. As they went down the corridor, Blake said in a low tone:

"Do you feel like coming on to Baker Street, general? I have made one or two discoveries back in these rooms, and I think we should lose no time in discussing them."

"Of course. I should be glad to. But I couldn't stick that bumptious ass any longer. I am most anxious to know why you thought to ask about that name, and —other things."

"I think I can promise to enlighten you considerably," rejoined Blake.

And no more was said until two stiff whiskies and a siphon of soda were standing on the heavy oak centre table in the consulting-room at Baker Street.

CHAPTER 5.   Sexton Blake's Logical Reasoning—The Baker Street Intruder—The Man Who Killed Count Torsky—Swift Nemesis.

"NOT only was Count Torsky murdered, general, but the garments he was wearing at the time were rifled and his personal luggage broken open and searched."

"What!"

"Yes."

"B-but how do you know this, Blake?"

"By seeing it. You heard me suggest to Inspector Thomas that he should make a search?"

"Yes."

"Well, that was the result. The lock of his trunk had been broken open and the leather round the lock of the suit-case cut by a sharp knife. I don't know what Count Torsky had in his luggage, but I do know that if there were any papers they were taken by the murderer, for I could not find a scrap."

"The scoundrel—the condemned scoundrel! We must do something to find him, Blake."

"I agree. But wait a moment, general, I do not believe it would do much good to question the reception clerk more closely. But there is one thing that makes me think the murder was possibly the work of the same people who killed the count's two companions at Marseilles."

"What gives you that idea?"

"On the left cheek I noticed some scratches. I asked the doctor if he had seen them, and he said he had—concluded they were the result of the fall."

"Yes. I heard that."

"Well, general, marks of that nature are one of the signs of the Cheka."

General Cotter brought his hand down hard on the arm of his chair.

"By heavens! You are right. I remember hearing that some place, but, of course, the Cheka wasn't in existence when I was in Russia."

"Do you recall that Count Torsky told us this morning that marks of the Cheka were also found on the bodies of his two companions?"

"Yes."

"Well, that is what caused me to look for something, because I already suspected that the same forces had annihilated the count. If this theory is correct, then what does it mean? It means that they are after something they know he has, or had, in his possession. In view of what he told me this morning I am very strongly of the opinion that this 'something' is nothing more nor less than the envelope he gave into my keeping."

"You are right!" exclaimed the general excitedly. "I am sure of it."

"Well, now, let us go a step further. If they knew he was staying at the Venetia, the probabilities are they followed him across from Paris, or, more likely, all the way from Marseilles. If I am correct in that surmise, then I think it safe to go a step further and say that it is quite on the cards they followed him when he went to see you last evening, and again when you and he came to see me this morning. In other words they knew that he first consulted you and then came to me. They would soon find out who you were, and likewise it would not take them long to discover who lives in this house."

"But he gave you the papers, if that is what they were after. Yet they killed him."

"They did not know he gave me the papers. They would figure that he would hardly do that at a preliminary interview. I think they would count on another appointment being made, and would think the count still had the papers in his possession. They must have had some reason to believe that certain documents in his possession would give them the clue as to the exact whereabouts of the gold bullion."

"You reason well, Blake. What you say is quite logical. I am quite bewildered. Give me an open foe to face or a military map to read, and I'll hold my own. But this killing in the dark and intrigue within intrigue is beyond me. What else? Is there no way we can run that scoundrel to earth?"

Blake lit a fresh cigarette and sipped his whisky.

"With luck—great luck—we might lay our hands on him. But if my former reasoning is correct, then I think our best plan is to wait until he comes to us."

Tinker, who was beginning to fathom what Blake was driving at, grinned behind his hand; but General Cotter only goggled at the detective.

"Come to us! No man would be such a fool!"

"He hasn't got those papers," said Blake quietly. "And I have. Take it from me, general, there are some very shrewd minds at work behind this, and I am convinced that when the murderer has time to examine all the objects he took from Count Torsky's pockets and luggage, and finds no signs of the documents he is seeking, then it won't take long for him to hit on the truth. If he does, then I shall most certainly be the next object of attack. That is what I meant when I said he might come to us."

"My sainted aunt! My good and sainted aunt! Your mind works about six jumps ahead of mine, Blake. I never thought of that. Do you really think so?"

"If my reasoning is sound then the odds are almost on that he will; if I am in error, then he won't. That is why I wanted you to come back to Baker Street. I could not discuss this phase of the affair before Inspector Thomas."

"I should say not. But what are you going to do?"

"I am going to give him the chance to come. And because I have a hunch he won't waste any time if that is his intention, I am going to watch for him to-night. It occurred to me that you might like to join in the vigil."

"Would I? I'm your man! Now we are getting to something where I can be of some use. Just tell me what you want me to do."

Blake glanced at his watch. It was just past midnight.

"The car is still at the kerb," he remarked. "If he is coming to-night he certainly won't come while it stands there. When I came in I took good care to see that the curtains of this room were closely drawn, and I do not believe the smallest chink of light can be seen from the street. But there is a light in the hall and that can be seen over the fanlight of the front door.

"Now my idea is that Tinker should take the car round to the garage. In the meantime you and I will discuss another whisky and soda, and when Tinker returns he can switch off the light in the hall. When that is done the whole front of the house will appear in darkness. Mrs. Bardell, my housekeeper, has, I know, been in bed this long while. Now out along, my lad, and remember to turn out the hall light when you return."

When Tinker had departed, Blake poured two more drinks, and then when he had lighted a fresh cigarette, went on:

"I do not think for a single moment that the fellow, if he does come, will attempt to enter by the front. If the place is being watched now he will see Tinker drive off in the car and will see him return. Then, when the lights go out he will think we have retired, unless he saw you come in, which might make him suspicious. However, that is something we shall have to risk.

"At any rate, if he does make the attempt he will give us time to retire and get to sleep, so he will hardly make the attempt before one o'clock or even later. And if he does he will come by the back. Now it is a warm night, hot in fact, and you will have noticed that there is a clear moonlit sky. We don't know how much time he has been able to spend here this evening even if he has been here at all. Not much at most, because it must have given him some bother to make his 'getaway' from the Venetia.

"Nevertheless, when he does come, he will try the back, I feel convinced, and in order to encourage him, I propose leaving the window of the laboratory partly open. He will not find it difficult to get over the wall at the back, and, once he comes up through the garden, he must see the open window. An active man can easily reach the windowsill of the laboratory from the ground. Tinker and I have often come that way when we wished to be unobserved. This is all speculation on my part, general, but I am going to play that hand to-night."

"Splendid. We all take up a position in the laboratory then?"

Blake coughed. He had expected this.

"Er—well, not exactly. You see he might come from the front, and it is just as necessary that we keep a watch here. So my plan is that you and Tinker shall remain here in the consulting-room. Those heavy curtains were made specially to prevent a single shaft of light being seen from the street, and there will be no need to turn off the light. I shall take up my place in the laboratory and then—well, then it is on the lap of the gods."

"I should prefer being with you there, Blake. But in this matter you are the commander and I am the soldier. I shall obey what you suggest."

Blake was relieved. He had expected the soldier to protest more emphatically. But it was just because he was a good soldier that the general had not done so. They heard a noise in the hall just then, and a few moments later Tinker came in.

"Did you turn out the light?" asked Blake.

"Yes, sir."

"Any signs of anyone hanging about?"

"Nothing that I could see, guv'nor."

"Did you take a look at the windows of this room?"

"Yes, sir. It was impossible to see a thing."

"Good. Is the sky still clear?"

"Yes, guv'nor, and the moon almost at the full."

"Then sit down, young 'un, and I will explain what the plan is."

He did so, and when Tinker understood that he and the general were to remain in the consulting-room while Blake went on guard in the laboratory, he looked as if he would like to protest vigorously; but a single glance from Blake caused him to change his mind.

Then they sat and talked in low tones until the hands of the clock pointed to one. As the silver chime struck, Blake rose and, opening a drawer in his desk, took out a small automatic and next a short length of supple-weighted leather which is commonly known as a "life-preserver."

He dropped the pistol into the side pocket of his coat and slung the life-preserver over his wrist by a loop that was attached to it after the fashion of the leather loop on a policeman's truncheon.

"I'll take up my post now," he said. "If you hear the sound of a shot or hear me shout, then come."

"You can count on that," returned the general grimly.

Blake turned to Tinker.

"See that General Cotter has what he wants, my lad." And with that he opened the door leading to the side hall, closed it gently after him and stole silently along towards his dressing-room. He entered that and changed his walking shoes for a pair of rubber-soled "sneakers"; then he slipped quietly into the laboratory.

The single window of the laboratory was directly opposite the door and on the left of the window, as Blake faced it, was a big, white-painted locker where were kept smocks, rubber coats, and other paraphernalia belonging to him and Tinker which they used when working at experiments. It was this cupboard which was Blake's immediate objective and, as there was sufficient moonlight to guide him, he did not attempt to bring his pocket-torch into play.

He paused only long enough to slide the lower sash of the window up about half-way and left the blind as it was. Then he opened the door of the locker and stepped inside, leaving the door open about half an inch or so in order to see and for ventilation.

By the time he was settled he heard a distant clock strike the quarter, and now and then a belated taxi hooted as it went along Baker Street. But for the rest it was as silent as the grave, and as he stood there peering out at the array of glass retorts and bottles, the weird shape of a white smock and cap on the wall and the round, goggling eyes of the two windows in the electric furnace, an eerie sensation came over him.

It was an odd experience for Blake to be hiding in a cupboard in his own house waiting for a murderer who might or might not come. He smiled to himself as he reflected the depth of hysterics into which Mrs. Bardell would plunge if she dreamed for a single moment what was afoot over her head.

The half hour struck. Still nothing happened. But Blake had plenty of patience. He had played the waiting game too often to spoil it by a premature withdrawal.

He had made up his mind that he would stick it until three o'clock, and if the fellow did not come by then, he would give it up for it would be getting daylight and the risk would be too great.

The three-quarter.

One distant taxi hooter was all that sounded as the last strokes of the church clock died away.

Slowly, deadly slow the minutes dragged by. By now the hanging smock and cap begun to get on Blake's nerves. He could almost imagine that some fiend of the night, moon-mad, had insinuated himself into them and was jeering at him. And the two "eyes" of the electric furnace seemed to have become alive. He realised that this was because he had been staring too fixedly into the room, and now he closed his eyes to give them relief and change the focus.

But scarcely had he done so when they flew open again, for, from immediately outside the locker, it seemed, had come a sound. Just one short scraping sound, that was all.

Instantly Blake was on the alert. Tensely he stood, scarcely breathing, listening with strained ears to catch a repetition of the sound. It did not come. What seemed like an eternity passed without anything happening. He started as the distant clock boomed the hour of two and then, just as the echo of the last chime died away, he saw a shadow streak across the narrow slit of the open door.

Someone had come in through the window.

Someone was standing half-way between the locker and the experimenting table. Blake started to press his fingers on the door to push it open; but suddenly he drew back as a shaft of light stabbed the half gloom of the laboratory. Here and there the beam went probing—up and down and across, stabbing once into the very slit of the open locker door until Blake thought he must be discovered. Then it was switched off as suddenly as it had come and Blake thought he heard a low mutter of some sort.

There was the scarcely perceptible sound of a footfall as the intruder started towards the door. And then Blake acted.

With one great heave he sent the door of the locker flying open. Even before it slammed he was out and half-way across to where the intruder had frozen in his tracks, appalled at this sudden apparition.

But only for a moment. Before Blake reached him he had hurled the pocket-torch full at the detective, catching him on the shoulder, and then there was a roar and a burst of flame almost blinding Blake as the other shot at close range.

It is a miracle how that shot missed Blake, but it did, and before the other could shoot a second time Blake had swung his life-preserver up and down with all his strength. There was a sickening thud as it caught the fellow on the side of his head. But it was not a knock-out, and before Blake could strike again the other was in at him.

Nothing loth, for he was certain now that he was dealing with the foul fiend who had murdered Count Torsky, Blake grappled with him, and at the first tensing of muscles knew he was up against a powerful antagonist.

He was wasting no time, however, in finesse. He was out to get this murderer, and get him quick, and so furious was his drive that both struggling figures went crashing across the room to fetch up against the experimenting table with terrific force.

Came a breakaway, and as he came out of the clinch Blake sent in a terrific right to the body, following with a hard smash to the jaw. The other shot back against the experimenting table as if he had been hit with a club, and his arms shot up wildly as he tried to grip something to keep him from falling.

In doing so he clutched at some of the bottles on the shelf above the experimenting table, and there was an uproar of breaking glass as he pulled half a dozen of the bottles down upon him.

Blake was ready to jump in again and deliver the coup de grace, but as the other flopped down among the heap of broken glass a pungent odour curled up, sending him back gasping and pawing at his mouth. He knew only too well what that odour was, and was just able to get his voice back in order to yell to Tinker and the general as they burst into the room.

"Back! Back!" he yelled. "Keep the general out, Tinker. The bottle of that deadly morsio poison is broken. Keep away. I'll try and get close enough to drag this fellow away."

Risking instant death—and, indeed, it is a wonder that he had not succumbed to that first whiff, for it was a poison that killed on one complete inhalation—Blake tried to creep forward and grasp the fallen man by the foot he forced himself to hold his breath, and when he thought his lungs would burst he managed to catch hold of one heel. A single desperate pull dragged the other away, and Blake kept on going until he reached the window.

There he paused long enough to push the window up the full way, and, lifting the limp figure in his arms, lowered him into the garden. So volatile was the marsio poison that Blake knew its fumes would be dissipated in a few minutes; but he knew, too, that until that time was passed it would be certain death to remain in the laboratory. He was half-groggy himself from the infinitesimal amount that had curled into his own nostrils, and had he breathed in just once, nothing, he knew, would have saved him.

That was why he had little hopes of resuscitating the man who lay at his feet, although he worked over him with as much energy as he would have devoted to a better cause. In the meantime Tinker and the general had dropped out of the dining-room window and had joined him, and, as Blake turned the limp body over, the general nodded his head.

"That's your man all right, Blake. A pure Slav type. By thunder, you were right! You have caught the man who murdered Torsky."

Blake straightened up.

"Well, he'll never murder anyone else," he said quietly. "He's done for. I'm sorry. I should like to have seen him go before a different judge, but it was his own fault. He caught at the shelf, and brought the whole lot down upon him."

"And a good job, too. What will you do with him?"

"Get him into the consulting-room and search him. Then I shall advise Inspector Thomas. After that it is up to the police, although I shall want a statement from you, general."

"Of course. I'll tell the commissioner just what happened. Let Tinker and me give you a hand."

Between them they lifted the body through the dining-room window, and carried it along to the consulting-room, where they laid it on the couch.

Then, with deft fingers, Blake went through the dead man's pockets, bringing to light a strange and heterogeneous collection of articles. There were many things there that, later on, proved beyond a doubt that the fellow was one of the secret emissaries of the Cheka.

But what interested Blake and the general and Tinker more than anything else were the various letters and papers of different kinds which bore the name of Count Torsky.

It was all the proof they needed that Torsky's murderer had been overtaken by a swift Nemesis.

[A Life Preserver circ 1927]

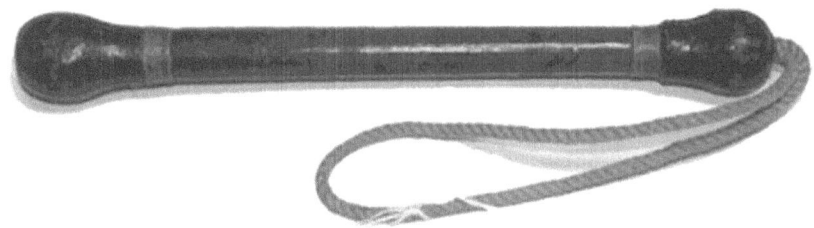

CHAPTER 6.   Blake and Tinker Cross to France—Extreme Secrecy—Huxton Rymer and Mary Trent Travel to Marseilles.

TWO days later Blake and Tinker left for Paris.

On the morning of the second day after the murder of Count Torsky a double inquest was held, and at this it was proved beyond a doubt that the man who had met his death in Blake's laboratory was the one who killed the young Russian.

On the basis of Blake's statement, Detective-inspector Thomas lost no time in ferreting out all the particulars possible about the murder. Among other papers found on him was a slip which made it appear that he had been staying at a small hotel in Soho since his arrival in London on the same evening when Count Torsky had come to the Venetia.

In his room there the inspector discovered documents which made it certain he had been a secret agent of the Cheka, but what was more important evidence, a pistol was discovered of the same calibre as that which must have caused the death of the count.

Moreover, when the bullet had been extracted from the latter's body, where it had lodged behind a rib at the back, it was found to be of Russian make, exactly similar to those which were found in the pistol.

Circumstantial evidence if you will, but sufficient to make it clear beyond any reasonable doubt that the murderer was the same who had crept into Blake's house that night.

The whole thing dovetailed too well. Taking first the murder of Torsky's two companions at Marseilles and the finding of the secret mark of the Cheka on them when they were found; then the trailing of the count to Paris and London; the giving of the name "Odjiska" as a password which would admit the murderer to the count's room (although only Blake, Tinker and General Cotter as yet knew the significance of that); the arrival in London the same evening that Count Torsky reached the Venetia; the swift action in the killing; then the visit to Blake's house—a move which the deductive mind of the detective had foreseen; and finally the discovery of many of Torsky's letters and papers on the person of the murderer together with the discoveries made by Inspector Thomas at the hotel in Soho.

There wasn't a single flaw in the whole chain of evidence, and, needless to say, Sexton Blake was held in no way to blame for what had happened in the laboratory. With regard to that incident General Cotter and Tinker were valuable witnesses.

Blake had a brief interview with the general before leaving London. It took place in the general's room at the War Office.

"So you are going to tackle it, Blake?" was the general's question.

Blake nodded.

"If I had any hesitation it vanished when Count Torsky was killed," he responded. "I am not sure who my principals are now, for the little band of patriots that started out on this crazy but courageous expedition are all dead so far as we know. But there are things in the documents which the count gave into my care which make me feel that I cannot abandon that gold to the Soviet. If I can get it out of Odjiska I shall do so. After that I shall have to try to find some means of delivering it to the person for whom it is intended."

"Technically the whole lot is yours if you can get it," mused the general.

But Blake shook his head.

"'I consider the recovery of that gold a sacred charge laid on me by the murder of Torsky. It will go to the person for whom those young men intended it if I can get it."

"What about finance?"

"Among the documents which Torsky entrusted to me there is one which will finance matters for the time being. If more money is required I shall put it up myself, and trust to fortune to get it back when the business is over."

"You are not a criminologist, Blake," blurted out the blunt military man. "You are a blessed altruist, a philanthropist."

Blake smiled.

"Not in the least, general. But I confess it galls me to think that the gold for which those young men gave their lives must fall into the hands of the gang which sits in the saddle in Russia to-day. I am no Tsarist; I don't care two straws who is in power in Russia except the Bolshevists. If they had attempted to rule honestly I should as soon have seen them there as any other party. But when one reflects how millions of little children have been debauched and sent adrift; when one reads actual figures of the hundreds of thousands who have been sacrificed, it makes one almost believe that high heaven has forgotten Russia. Men in the throes of revolution—yes; but little children—no!

And that is why I am going after that gold!"

"By heavens! I'd like to come with you," exploded the other.

"And I'd like to have you, general. But this is a game which only an outsider can play; it must be played with a free hand—and you are tied."

"Worse luck, I am. But if there is anything I can do in an unofficial way you know you have only to call on me."

"I am sure of that."

Shortly after that Blake took his departure, and before midnight that night he and Tinker were in Paris. Blake's actual destination was Marseilles, but before proceeding to the southern port he had a few things to attend to in Paris. His chief concern was to try to get in touch with someone connected with the organisation for which Torsky had been acting.

He could not approach the Grand Duke Nicholas direct, for reasons which are obvious. But Blake knew the secret ways of Paris quite as well as he knew those of London, and although it took three days of slow and cautious probing he at last found the man he was seeking.

That individual, a former colonel in the Tsarist army, was as cautious as a cat at first; but when, in his room at the Carlitz, in the Rue de Rivoli, Blake gave him undeniable proof that he had been in the confidence of the ill-fated count, the Russian thawed, and before they parted there was a complete understanding between them.

He urged Blake to make use of their branch organisation in Marseilles and, while Blake accepted a confidential letter of introduction to the head of the branch, he had no intention of using it. He was remembering what had happened to Torsky's two companions, and he still believed there had been a traitor somewhere in that organisation.

The question of finance was gone into, and satisfactory arrangements arrived at.

Following the interview, Blake made a private visit to his intimate friend, Monsieur Dupuis, the prefect of police. Through that influential personage he secured certain papers which covered every need of the character he intended assuming—for he had already formed a tentative plan in London.

He was also given papers for Tinker, and that same evening they shifted their quarters to a small hotel in the Latin Quarter.

The following night when they arrived at the Gare de Lyons to take the train to Marseilles Sexton Blake and Tinker had completely vanished so far as appearances went. Instead, there was a typical-looking seafaring man of the French type, dressed in blue pilot coat and trousers, and wearing a peaked French cap with soft, floppy top such as every French tramp skipper wears. There was also the regulation black beard and moustache—a masterpiece which Blake had had fitted at Durands, the famous Parisian wig maker and theatrical outfitter.

As for Tinker, he looked as if he might be either an apprentice or a young wireless operator, and certainly anyone observing them would have felt quite certain that they were just what they appeared.

Never in his life had Blake taken more care with a disguise, for he knew that they were indeed venturing into the jaws of the black tiger.

Even their own luggage had been stored at the Carlitz, and the bags they had with them were typically French. Not a single detail had Blake forgotten, and before many days had passed he was to congratulate himself on his foresight.

They reached the station some twenty minutes before the train was due to leave, and when they had deposited the bags in a second-class compartment they strolled up and down the platform to make the most of the balmy August evening.

They had made a dozen turns or so when suddenly Blake felt Tinker clutch his arm, and, as he turned his head in the direction of the door through which the passengers were coming, he scarcely suppressed a start on recognising two persons who hurried through the press on the heels of a porter and disappeared into one of the wagon lits.

It was Dr. Huxton Rymer and Mary Trent.

They had neither of them seen the pair from Baker Street, and even if they had it would have made no difference, for their disguises were too complete for them to have the slightest fear of discovery.

Blake continued to the end of the refreshment-room, then he signed to the lad to turn, and this time they walked along until they came abreast of the sleeping car through the windows of which they could see Rymer standing in the door of one of the compartments.

A little further on they caught sight of Mary Trent instructing the porter how to arrange her luggage; then they were past and walked on until they reached the engine.

"Where do you suppose they are off to, guv'nor?" whispered Tinker when he saw there was no one near.

"I haven't an idea," breathed Blake. "But don't discuss it now. If we are lucky enough to have our compartment to ourselves we can talk it over later."

They paced up and down until within a few minutes of the time of starting. On re-entering their compartment they found to their satisfaction that, so far, no one else had chosen it, and Blake took the liberty of closing the door as a slight discouragement to any belated passenger who might arrive. But no one disturbed them, and when they finally drew out they were alone.

Ordinarily Blake would have chosen to travel in the wagon lits for such a long journey, but no ordinary French tramp skipper would have dreamed of squandering money on such "foolishness," and in keeping with his role, he thought it wiser to stick to the second-class.

If they could keep the compartment to themselves it wouldn't be so bad, for each could stretch out on one of the seats, and after all they are, for all practical purposes, as comfortable as a bunk in a sleeping car.

When they were clear of Belleville and the southern suburbs Blake lit a cigarette and remarked:

"Rymer and Mary Trent travelling south—probably Marseilles, Tinker. Our friend must be off on some new stunt. He doesn't usually travel abroad except for two reasons—one to escape the too pressing attentions of Scotland Yard, and the other to pull off a new job. I'd like to know what he is up to this time."

"Well, he's got his partner with him, anyway, guv'nor."

Blake nodded.

"Yes; when she travels with him there is usually something in the wind. If they are going as far as Marseilles we'll just keep an eye on them to see what they get up to."

Early the next morning when they stepped out on to the platform at Marseilles, they delayed with their luggage long enough to watch what passengers got out of the sleeping car.

Blake was by no means surprised to see Rymer and Mary Trent among them, and when it was plain that they were going into the town instead of changing to one of the Riviera trains he gave a sign to Tinker.

"Go after them. You'll find me in front of the Bourse in an hour's time. I'll find a place for us to put up."

Tinker slouched off as if he was at a loose end, while Blake followed a porter to the gates. He had in mind a place near the new basin, which he knew to be a rendezvous for skippers and mates of small tramps, and he was hoping he would be able to find quarters there, for it would suit his role perfectly.

He could not remember the number, but he knew it was next to a cafe known as the Rotonde, and it was this which he gave as the address.

Just before reaching the cafe he saw the place he had in mind, and rapped on the window for the taxi to draw up. Bidding the man wait he mounted the steps of the lodging-house, a rather dingy-looking place, and rang the bell.

Madame herself answered the door, and briefly Blake stated his wants. It seemed that madame could oblige him with two rooms, if he would care to see them. He did choose to do so, and although they lacked to a vast extent the first essential of cleanliness, he decided to take them.

He carried his own luggage, after paying off the taxi, and when he had settled matters by paying a week in advance, and telling madame that one of his ship's company would occupy the second room, he filled his pipe.

Before walking along to the Bourse, which wasn't very far distant, he stopped at the cafe for coffee and a croissant. He figured that Tinker would be at least half an hour, and so far only twenty minutes had gone by since they parted at the railway station.

Another quarter of an hour went by before Blake found himself in front of the Bourse which, though smaller, is somewhat similar to that in Paris. Almost the first person he saw was Tinker, and he knew by the cheerful grin on the lad's face that he had some news to impart.

"Well, what's happened to them?" asked Blake when they were walking along.

"It was too easy, guv'nor. They drove straight to the docks and went, on board the P. & O. boat M—. I managed to get a squint at the labels which were put on their luggage, and they were stamped 'Port Said.'"

"Port Said. That means they may be going to Cairo, or possibly will be changing there for some other port up the Levant coast. I wonder what game Rymer is chasing this time. However, it doesn't matter to us. We can't follow shadows; there is too much reality to face."

"Unless he is on the same wheeze," remarked Tinker.

But Blake shook his head.

"I don't think so, my lad. If Rymer has been in England for some time past—or even in Paris, I don't see how he could get wind of that. I have succeeded in getting rooms of a sort which will serve our purpose, although I could wish them cleaner. I will show you the place, and, while I have no objection to your prowling about the town if you wish, I want to caution you not to get into conversation with anyone. Do you understand?"

"Sure, guv'nor! I won't speak to a soul. What are you going to do?"

"Take the first step in the plan I formed in London."

They walked back along the water front, past the new basin, and then up the Cannebiere until they passed the Rotonde. At the next house Blake mounted the steps, using the latchkey which madame had given him after he had paid a week's money in advance.

He left Tinker in the room which had been allotted to him, and with a renewal of the caution started out again.

Blake's destination was the offices of an old and highly respected firm of commission agents—Messrs. Pichot, de Gasquet & Rennecon, with one of the partners of which he had had dealings in the past. Their place of business was near the Bourse on the second floor of an old building, and as soon as he had mounted the stairs to the waiting-room Blake sent in his name to M. Rennecon, the partner in question.

That gentleman was seated at the desk in his bureau dictating letters, and of course he looked up with no sign of recognition as "Captain Beaumont" (the name which Blake had sent in) entered. But he dismissed his secretary and received Blake courteously enough.

Blake had debated whether to disclose his identity to M. Rennecon or not, but had finally decided not to do so for the present, at least. This precaution was but a part with the general secrecy which he considered essential to the success of his plan. But he did decide to use his own name as an introduction.

So after he was seated and had laid his peaked cap on the floor, he pressed the tips of his fingers together and began.

"It seems odd, monsieur, that I, a French sea captain, should have received your name from an Englishman. But so it is. I was informed by this gentleman that you could probably manage certain business for me."

"Alors, monsieur, and the name of this Englishman?"

"Monsieur Blake—Monsieur Sexton Blake, of London."

Rennecon looked frankly surprised.

"Monsieur Sexton Blake! It is true, monsieur, that I know Monsieur Blake quite well. He is a man with whom it has always been a great pleasure to do business."

Blake inclined his head as if he, too, had found Monsieur Blake a pleasant person in his dealings.

"And what can I do for you, monsieur?" went on Rennecon. "It will be a pleasure to be of assistance to a friend of Monsieur Blake's."

"I am in need of two things, monsieur— a ship and a cargo. For the ship I am prepared to charter, but not to buy; for the cargo I am prepared to pay spot cash in the form of a sterling draft on London."

What is the nature of the cargo you seek, monsieur?"

"Tin plate."

(Before leaving London Blake had taken the trouble to inquire of a large firm of exporters in the city what would be a desirable cargo to ship through on speculation to the Crimea, and had promptly been informed that either tin plate or fertilizers were in steady demand in that market.)

"Tin plate. I think it would be possible to secure a cargo of tin plate here in Marseilles, monsieur, but it would be necessary for me to inquire. We have not done any business in that commodity for some time past, and I am a little out of touch with the movements of stocks and prices. Are you in a .great hurry?"

"I do not wish to waste time, but I do not desire to be precipitate. I might also mention, monsieur, that, failing a full cargo of tin plate, I should be prepared to mix that cargo with fertilizer in bags."

"Ah! I can meet you there. We do a large business in fertilizers, monsieur, and it would be a matter of only a few moments for me to give you the latest quotations if you will indicate the sort you require. Pardon, monsieur, but perhaps if you will tell me for what port—"

"I am indulging in a speculation, monsieur. I have been informed on excellent authority that a cargo of that nature would fetch good prices in Odessa or other ports in South Russia, providing one was on the spot and could make immediate delivery."

Rennecon nodded his head.

"As for fertilizers, you are quite right. There is an excellent market there at present; and if that is your destination I can recommend the kind that is most suitable for your purpose. Nitrates and phosphates are in greatest demand."

"I would not object to a few thousand bags, monsieur, but I should like at least a portion of the cargo to be tin plate."

"I am sure I can arrange that for you, and you can depend that I shall do so at the very best market price. What is your limit, monsieur?"

"Twenty thousand pounds is the amount of the sterling draft I have. I am prepared to invest it all."

Rennecon made a few calculations on a slip of paper, then he nodded his head.

"It will not cover a large cargo, monsieur, for tin plate is an expensive commodity. But I could make up a mixed lot which would give you enough for, say, a vessel of eight hundred or a thousand tons."

"That is about the size I have in mind. But I have yet to find the craft. Can you be of assistance to me there, monsieur?"

"I am but we never touch charters direct. Our charters are all handled by a gentleman who specialises in that and in outfitting. I can take you to him if you wish. It is Monsieur Michel Bompard, whose offices are not far from here."

"I should be deeply obliged if you would do so, monsieur. But first I shall, if you please, place my draft in your hands for safe keeping."

As he spoke Blake drew out a duplicate draft or, rather, letter of credit on a well-known London bank for the sum of twenty thousand pounds sterling. When this had been duly placed in the safe and a receipt given to Captain Beaumont, Monsieur Rennecon rose, and, taking up his hat, escorted his visitor out of the office.

It was, as he had said, but a short walk to the business premises of Monsieur Bompard, and they were fortunate enough to find that gentleman in his office.

He greeted Monsieur Rennecon with every consideration, for the latter's firm were valued clients, and for this reason he was effusive to the stranger who was introduced and vouched for by Monsieur Rennecon.

In a few words the commission agent explained what his companion's requirements were, and as Monsieur Bompard has already appeared in this record (though that appearance was some days later for Rymer and Mary Trent were then only on their way to Port Said to see Halloran) it can be understood that he immediately assured Captain Beaumont that he could find him just the sort of craft he was looking for.

He inquired naturally for what purpose it was required, and it was the commission agent who told him it was a round trip charter to the Black Sea. Bompard did not admit to them that only a short time before he had been in negotiation with other clients for a similar charter, but it was he to whom Count Torsky had gone, although Blake was unaware of that. There had been no reference to Bompard in the documents which Torsky had given him.

It was arranged that Monsieur Bompard should look round that very morning and see what was available, and he promised to communicate with Captain Beaumont some time during the afternoon.

Blake accordingly gave him the address at which he was living, and after a few more compliments he and Rennecon departed.

Monsieur Rennecon parted from Blake near the Bourse, for he was anxious to find out how the tin plate market stood, and Blake, not ill-pleased with his morning's work, hailed a taxi and instructed the man to drive to the offices of the commandant of the port, for he had a private letter from the prefect in Paris to deliver to that gentleman.

CHAPTER 7. The Treachery of Monsieur Bompard—The Agent of the Cheka.

ALTHOUGH Monsieur Bompard had promised Blake that his first care would be to find out what cargo tramps were available for charter, he did not keep that promise to the letter.

Instead of proceeding to the informal exchange where such matters were arranged, he made his way along the harbour front by the old basin until he came to a dingy-looking cafe whose habitues, even at that hour of the morning, did not present a very wholesome appearance.

But this worried Monsieur Bompard not at all. He passed through the outer room, giving a brief nod to the "patron" as he went by, and entering an inner room, paused to gaze about him.

Apparently he was in search of someone, and it was evident that the individual he sought was not there, for he turned and lifted one eyebrow ever so slightly at the "patron."

Scarcely a soul would have noticed the signal which the "patron" gave, but Bompard caught it, for immediately he continued on through the inner room and through a door which led to a courtyard at the back. There a flight of wooden stairs led to a floor above, and Bompard mounted these. He rapped lightly on a door at the top, then pushed it open and stepped into a room which was practically a replica of the inner room beneath.

There were few customers in the place— half a dozen or so in all; but the man Bompard sought was there, seated alone at a table in one corner drinking what Bompard knew to be vodka. That particular drink would not have been served in the cafe below.

Bompard made his way to the table and seated himself facing the other. This individual was a dark, low-browed man with close-set, cunning eyes and a straggling black beard. He had the appearance of one who would look more at ease in the coarse garb of a peasant, but his clothes were quite as good as those of the Frenchman.

In brief he was one of those anomalies which one finds in power in Russia to-day— an ignorant peasant, who through sheer cunning has forged into the inner councils of the Soviet and the dreaded Cheka; a boor, a bully to those beneath him, and a fawning sycophant to those above him. A creature with scores of murders to his credit, or, rather, discredit, and one of those who waded through blood to power in Moscow during the early days of the last revolution.

At present he was one of the foreign secret agents of the Cheka, and as such was one of the most dangerous mad dogs let loose. But he had unlimited funds at his command, and that was of chief interest to Bompard, who had already tapped that free-flowing spring.

The Russian spoke French shockingly, but it was sufficient for the agile mind of Bompard to grasp what be said, and, moreover, his experiences in Russia had taught him to speak without moving his lips, which made it practically impossible to overhear him even at the next table, and there were three empty tables between him and the next which was occupied. The occupant of that was one of his own spies.

"Well?" he asked curtly in a voice that was thick with the fiery liquor he had been drinking. "What brings you here?"

"I have news for you," answered Bompard in a low tone.

"News, is it? I have had a fill of news today. Things have been happening in London, my friend. Is that your news?" (He had evidently just heard from someone in London that while his agent had killed Count Torsky he himself had paid the death penalty. And he was in no pleasant mood considering that he was no nearer than before to getting possession of the documents which Torsky had carried.) Bompard shook his head.

"I know nothing of any news from London. My news is of Marseilles, and I think it may interest, you."

"Curses and hades! What is it?"

Bompard spread out his hands.

"Our little arrangement, monsieur," he purred. "Are you forgetting?"

"Ho! So you don't even give me news without being paid."

"I must live, monsieur."

"Curses and hades! If I had you in Moscow you wouldn't live long!"

"But we are in France, monsieur," rejoined Bompard coolly. He was no coward for all his crookedness, was Bompard, and, besides, he knew something about the two Russians whose bodies had been found floating in the harbour. One anonymous whisper to the prefect and—

"Well, how much is it this time?"

"I consider the information is worth ten thousand francs," was Bompard's reply.

"Ten thousand devils! Are you crazy? Do you think my skin is made of money?"

Bompard shrugged and snapped his fingers at a waiter. He ordered an innocuous syrup, and when it was brought sipped it leisurely. He knew he had the other where he wanted him, and he was prepared to wait. Nor was there any question of haggling. If his price wasn't paid then, all right. He would keep his information to himself.

The Russian glared at him in silent rage for some minutes; then he banged his fist on the table.

"Very well! I pay! But if your news isn't worth it I'll gouge out your insides and feed them to the fish in the harbour."

"The news!" snarled the other. "Out with it!"

"The money!" mimicked Bompard. "Out with it, monsieur!"

There was another silent battle between them, but the higher intelligence of Bompard won. If they had been in Russia it would have been different. But here—

The Russian, after a suspicious look round, thrust his hand inside his waistcoat and drew out a wad of thousand franc notes that made Bompard's eyes glisten and his tongue grow dry. Michel Bompard would have sold every mortal thing on earth for money.

Laboriously the Russian thumbed off ten of the notes and pushed them across.

"There!" he mumbled. "Now out with it!"

Bompard carefully counted the money before placing it in his own pocket. When that little formality had been complied with he finished the remains of his syrup and then bent over the table.

"Monsieur," he said in a voice that was scarcely more than a whisper, "there are others inquiring for a ship to go to the Crimea."

The Slav breathed heavily as his little eyes fixed Bompard's.

"The same," he muttered.

"No. I do not know who is behind it. But I had a visitor this morning. He is looking for a return charter, a small cargo tramp, to go to the Crimea and return."

"Is he Russian?"

"No. He is, I believe, French."

"How did he come to you?"

"He was brought to me by a very respectable merchant here with whom I have done much business in the past. That merchant could not be mixed up in—you know what."

"Does he want to charter immediately?"

"He seems in haste."

"What about a cargo?"

"My friend attends to that. There was some mention of fertilizers and tin plate."

"Fertilizers and tin plate are used in the Crimea," muttered the Russian.

"Quite so, and the whole thing may be just as it appears. But I thought you might wish to know. You said you desired information of every ship which cleared for the Black Sea."

"And this man is a stranger to you?"

"But surely. I have never seen him before. But he is French, and mentioned that his papers were French."

"He was alone?"

"Oui."

"Have you his address?"

"But yes. He gave it to me. I am to communicate with him this afternoon."

"At what time?"

"None was stated."

"Could you get him to your office about four o'clock?"

"It is possible."

"Give me his address."

Bompard took out the paper on which he had written Captain Beaumont's address. He had no need to retain it, for he knew the place well enough. The other read it laboriously and stuffed it into his pocket.

"Where is this place?"

"Do you know the Rotonde cafe?"

"Off the Cannebiere—yes, I know it."

"It is next door to that."

"I will find it."

"What will you do?"

"I don't know, but it doesn't matter to you. You get this man at your office at four o'clock. I'll attend to the rest. Curses and hades!— Fertilizers and tin plate! What next? If you secure a charter for him let me know at once."

Bompard smiled.

"On our usual agreement, of course."

"Curses and hades, yes! Now get off about your business."

Bompard, quite satisfied, rose, and with a suave bow departed. He had his own inward opinion of the hog at the table, and had many times apostrophised him by many choice and insulting epithets—to himself.

As long as the money flowed freely he would not become articulate. There was plenty of time for that should it become advisable. And, besides, there was always that little hint which could be passed on to the prefect.

When he was gone the Cheka agent sat in moody silence for the better part of half an hour. Then suddenly he lifted his head and gave a sharp "click" with his tongue. At the sound the man who was seated a few tables away rose and joined him.

They talked in Slav, a low peasant form of the patois, for a considerable time, and once the Cheka agent drew out the paper which Bompard had given him and showed it to the other. Following that the man rose and took his departure, while the one who remained ordered more vodka.

CHAPTER 8.   Tinker Guards the Den—The Armed Intruder—Sexton Blake's Suspicions.

SEXTON BLAKE and Tinker lunched al the Rotonde. After, they took a stroll along the Cannebiere, but as Blake was anxious to be on hand should any word come through from Rennecon or Bompard, they soon returned to their lodgings.

As they entered, they noticed that madame was talking with a man in the lower hall, but as they took him to be one of her seafaring tenants they paid no attention to the matter. Blake's room being the largest, they sat there talking until past three o'clock, when madame knocked at the door and handed "Captain Beaumont" a letter.

It was from Monsieur Bompard, who informed Captain Beaumont that he had been making inquiries and thought he had found a ship that would suit his client's purpose.

He would be glad if Captain Beaumont could find it possible to call at his offices at four o'clock, when they could, if Captain Beaumont wished, go and inspect the craft in question.

Scarcely had Blake finished reading the epistle when there was another knock at the door, and once more madame entered, bearing another letter. This proved to be from Monsieur Rennecon, who begged Captain Beaumont to call during the afternoon if convenient, as he had ascertained the information he required.

Blake rose at once.

"I'll go along now, young 'un. I may be some time, what with Rennecon and Bompard. You can do what you please, but I'd stick round fairly close if I were you."

Tinker yawned.

"It's too darned hot to go mooching about," he said, "and as I'd look queer using a taxi in this get-up, I think I'll take a nap."

"All right—a good idea,"

When Blake had departed Tinker went into his own room, and, slipping off his shoes, drew the blind. He lay down on the bed, and almost before he knew it had dropped off to sleep. How long he slept he could not have told; but suddenly and, as far as he knew, for no reason at all, he was wide awake.

He sat up in bed and slid to the floor, yawning. He drew up the blind, and saw that while the sun was getting low it was still afternoon. A glance at his watch showed him it was just a quarter-past five, so he had slept a little more than an hour. He knew Blake could not have returned, or he would have come in to tell him how things had gone.

He sat on the side of the bed musing about the new adventure on which they had embarked, and thinking with some pleasure that it would be rather jolly to voyage into the Black Sea in their craft, even if it did prove to be a dingy tramp.

It had been some time since he and Blake had been at Odessa, and Tinker had never seen Odjiska, though Blake had been there once before.

From that his thoughts wandered to Rymer and Mary Trent. He had been more curious than Blake to know what they could be up to this time, but, like Blake, he figured that Rymer must have some game on in Egypt, though it was an off-time of the year to find any very rich pickings there. Still, one never knew what schemes Rymer might be following.

Then someone sneezed.

That was all—a trivial thing one might say. And so it would have appeared to Tinker, but for the fact, that he was positive it had come from Blake's room.

Had Blake, then, returned? he asked himself. If so, it was odd that he hadn't come in to wake him up. And if it wasn't Blake, who was it? It couldn't be madame, for it had been a man's sneeze.

He slid off the bed softly. Next he tiptoed to the door in his socks, and laying his fingers on the handle turned it slowly. He drew the door open ever so gently and stepped into the hall.

It was only a step to the door of Blake's room, and, when he reached it, he stood close to the panel, listening.

He was almost certain he could hear someone moving about inside, stealthily it seemed to Tinker. Bending down, he applied one eye to the keyhole, and a few moments later something came between him and the light from the window.

There was someone in the room! Was it Blake?

He took hold of the handle with infinite precaution and began to turn. Slowly, ever so slowly, he flexed his wrist until he had given a full half-twist. Then he heaved his shoulder against it and sent it crashing inwards.

A startled curse greeted his intrusion. The man who had been bending over Blake's trunk, which was lying open, with half the contents scattered on the floor came up sharply and swung, clawing at his hip-pocket even as he did so.

Tinker had just time to see that he was the same swarthy-looking individual who had been talking to madame when he and Blake came in from lunch before he dashed forward.

He did not attempt to come into ordinary grips. He knew from that gesture of the hand that the fellow was armed, and the expression in his eyes plainly told that he would shoot, and shoot to kill. With no weapon, there was only one thing Tinker could do.

Lowering his head he drove straight in to the other's stomach with all his force. The other crashed back against, the end of the bed with a grunt, and, catching hold of one leg, Tinker flipped him on to the floor.

Then he was down on him, one knee in the small of his back and one arm dragged up between his shoulder-blades. The whole thing was a combination of a rough and tumble, a football tackle and jiu-jitsu, but it served for the time being.

The intruder struggled frantically until Tinker increased the pressure on his arm, causing such an excruciating pain that the other subsided with a groan of agony.

"You stay where you are!" snarled Tinker. (And it says a good deal for the lad's presence of mind, under such conditions, that he did not forget to speak in French.) "If you don't, I'll break your arm clean. Do you understand?"

A smothered moan answered him as he applied still more pressure to emphasise his threat, and then, still holding his grip ruthlessly, he searched about for some means to secure his prisoner,

But suddenly he recollected that the other had a weapon, so, first, he thrust his free hand into his hip-pocket and dragged out a heavy automatic-pistol. He flung this on to the bed, and, as he did so, caught sight of the two heavy straps which had been round Blake's trunk, and which the other had unbuckled when he forced the lock.

With a deft movement, Tinker got hold of the buckle-end of one and began dragging it towards him. A sudden squirm on the part of his prisoner warned him that he was unconsciously loosing his pressure, so he was forced to desist until he had given a more vicious twist to the arm than before.

He had no intention of snapping the bone, but he was determined to keep his man as he had him, and it was only when there was a distinct "snap" and a sharp yell of pain from the man under him that he realised that the job was done.

Still he hung on, and this time he managed to drag the strap free from beneath the trunk. Relinquishing his hold of the broken arm he dragged the other up between the shoulder-blades, and, this time, when he repeated his threat, his prisoner knew there was no bluff.

He lay quiescent while Tinker got the strap under him and round; then he repeated the process, for there was plenty of length, and when he slipped the tongue through the buckle, he dragged it down tight, although he did have heart enough to go easy on the broken arm.

This done, he caught hold of the other strap and wound it round the fellow's legs, clinching it even tighter than the other. Then he rolled his prisoner over on his back, and was just getting to his feet, when there was a sound at the door, and he swung sharply to see Blake standing on the threshold.

"Que es ce que e'est?" he demanded, or, rather, thundered.

With his back to the bound intruder, Tinker gave an almost imperceptible wink. Then:

"I found him here, mon capitain," he answered. "When you departed, mon capitain, I lay down for a little. I woke suddenly, and, hearing sounds in here, thought you had returned. I came to see, mon capitain, and, on opening the door, discovered this apache going through your trunk. He tried to shoot, mon capitain; his weapon is on the bed. But I was too quick for him and—his arm is broken."

Blake came into the room and closed the door. Walking across, he stood gazing down at the prisoner, a heavy and threatening frown on his brow. With his black beard and moustache he looked sinister enough just then.

"You are the man who was talking to madame when we came in this afternoon!" he snarled suddenly. "What were you doing in my room? No lies, or I'll break more than your arm for you!"

The fellow looked away and mumbled something. Well he knew what his fate would be if he should betray his master. So, after being urged by the point of Blake's boot, he whimpered a long, rambling tale about being a seaman out of employment, and had succumbed to temptation.

Blake heard him out, knowing full well that he was telling a tissue of lies. When he had finished, he bent down, and with a practised hand went through his clothes, even feeling beneath his waistcoat. He brought out quite an assortment of articles, but they were only those which might have been found on any man of his type, and not a scrap of writing among the lot.

When he had assured himself of this, Blake walked to the door and opened it. There was no bell so, making his way to the head of the stairs he bellowed in stentorian tones for madame. After several attempts there came a shrill reply from the bowels of the building, and presently the stout madame appeared, puffing, and in a state of agitation to know what was wrong.

"I want you to come to my room, madame," said Blake curtly.

She came up the stairs heavily, a look of concern on her face, for withal she had to be hard-hearted at times, she was a good soul at heart and she had taken a decided fancy to this tall, grim-faced skipper who paid his way in advance.

"Monsieur, monsieur, what is it?" she panted.

"This way, madame, please," was the only reply Blake vouchsafed.

He led the way back to his bed-room, and when he stood aside so that madame could see the bound prisoner on the floor, she gave a yelp and threw up her hands. Then she recognised the new tenant who had only come that day, and broke into a torrent of Provencal patois that not even Blake could follow. When she had calmed down somewhat Blake related briefly what Tinker had told him.

"He is no sailor man, madame," he said in conclusion. "He is a common thief. He came to your respectable house but to steal."

Blake's words drove the good soul into a fury, and with arms waving like a windmill, she broke into a fresh torrent of words. But this time it was abuse, and when a woman of Provence lets herself go it is something worth hearing, or something to fly from, depending on how one looks at it.

Tinker almost caught himself grinning, but Blake's face was as hard as granite. When madame paused, because she had run out of breath and vocabulary at the same time, he nodded his approval.

"What you say is all true," he said. "And now, what shall we do with this canaille?"

"The police—a cell—oh! But for the galleys again!" she cried. "I would give him a stretch there that would blister him, I assure you."

Blake nodded his approval once more; but he had very good reason why he did not want a police matter made of it. He had used his secret letter from M. Dupuis with the port commandante, but he did not desire to come into contact with the police unless it was absolutely necessary. That was for a last resort, and he was still sticking to the close incognito he had set himself and Tinker.

"He deserves that and more," he remarked. "On the other hand, he was discovered before he could steal anything. Moreover, mon petit took his weapon away from him, and then in the struggle broke the right arm with which he would have stolen. It is a good punishment, and, madame, I would not have your house become notorious through me."

Madame—who had a sudden vision of being taken to court as a witness; of the police prowling about seeking evidence, and of the crowds on the terrace of the Rotonde, saying: "Oh, ho! So Madame Claudio is caught by the police! What has she been up to?"—began to see there was wisdom in what Blake said.

"But you, monsieur le capitain?" she ventured tentatively.

Blake shrugged.

"I shall be satisfied if I never see him again. If I had him aboard my ship I'd give him the rope's end, I promise you. But I shall be satisfied if you give me leave to kick him down the front steps into the street."

"You may, and with pleasure, monsieur le capitain."

"See that the way is clear, mon petit," ordered Blake, giving the lad a significant look at the same time. "I shall go along to this thief's room, madame, and see if there is any stolen property in his luggage. He will be quite safe here."

"And I will come with you, monsieur."

Tinker had left the room, and now Blake and madame went along to the one which had been given to the new tenant. There was a cheap valise on the floor which was not locked, and on opening it Blake found nothing except an old suit and a pair of rubber-soled shoes.

"He had those for use at night," he remarked, holding them up. "Well, he will use them elsewhere, madame."

Carrying the bag out he tossed it down into the lower hall, and then, as they went back to his room, he caught sight of Tinker slipping out of his own room where he had been putting on his shoes and making for the stairs.

Blake gave the lad time enough to get out on to the street and at a point of vantage before dragging the prisoner to his feet and releasing him. Then catching him by the collar he forced him along the hall and down the stairs to the door which Tinker had left open.

Madame stood by to watch, and clicked her tongue with complete approval as Blake, sparing nothing, kicked the fellow with such force that he shot down the steps and clean across the pavement, a spectacle for the curious who were gathered on the terrace of the Rotonde for the aperetif hour. After him went the valise, and then Blake closed the door.

"My husband could never have done that," remarked madame sentimentally.

But at this advance Blake thought it time to fade away, which he did.

He returned to his room and made a careful inventory of his belongings. Nothing was missing, and, indeed, it would not have mattered very much if there was. He had been too careful to leave himself open in that way.

Every shred of clothing in the trunk was marked with the initials 'A. B.', which were supposed to stand for 'Alphonse Beaumont,' and what few letters there were bore the same name—fake letters which he had written in Paris and posted from one side of the city to a small hotel in the Latin Quarter where he and Tinker had stayed just before coming south.

But he realised then how near discovery he would have been had he not thought of those minute details.

Blake filled his pipe—thanking his lucky stars that this, at least, was a habit that was growing rapidly among the French —and, seating himself, sank into deep thought. He sent his mind back to London, and beginning there from the moment when General Cotter had brought Count Torsky to Baker Street, he went over every single item which he could recall —and Blake forgot little.

From London he brought his examination of memory to Paris, and after a comprehensive survey of his movements there, finally arrived back at Marseilles, he had just reached this point when the door opened and Tinker came in. Blake looked at him inquiringly.

"I spotted him as soon as you kicked him out, guv'nor. He was too much upset to think that anyone might be spying on him. He hailed the first cab that came along, a *fiacre*, and jumped in. Then he forgot his valise and the driver had to get down and get it for him. I risked a taxi, and followed along slowly. The fiacre drew up in front of a dingy-looking cafe on the water-front—a place called the Cafe Cigogne—and he went in there. I thought he might be going in for a drink to pull himself together, but he was there so long I figured he intended staying, so I thought I had better come back here and report. My word, you certainly booted him out. He went across the pavement as if he had been shot from a catapult."

Blake paid no attention to the last of Tinker's remarks.

"The Cafe Cigogne," he muttered. "I know the place, near the old basin; and not a very savoury place at that."

He was silent for a little, then: "I have been thinking, young 'un.

"I have been going over in my mind every small incident that has happened since General Cotter came to Baker Street that morning. But I am positive this business of this afternoon did not have its inception in London.

"We don't know if the man who murdered Count Torsky had any companions or not; but I am inclined to think he was playing a lone hand. At any rate, we could not have been more cautious in leaving London, and even if we were followed I am positive we covered our tracks completely in Paris. As ourselves, we entirely vanished there, and I do not believe a single soul, with the exception of Monsieur Dupuis, could know that Captain Beaumont and his companion were the pair who left London. Luckily, I attended to such minor, but none the less important, details as marks on our clothes and so on."

"Then you think this thing that happened this afternoon has to do with the other, guv'nor?"

"I strongly suspect so. That man was no more an ordinary prowling thief than you or I. I am convinced that he came here to-day for the sole purpose of getting at my luggage. I do not believe, when he came, that he knew you were with me. Hence his nerve in entering my room as soon as he saw me safely away. No. In my opinion it has had its inception in Marseilles."

"Here!" exclaimed Tinker. "But how could that be, sir?"

"That is the mystery. Since our arrival this morning I have spoken to only two persons aside from madame and the garcon at the Rotonde. And I take it you have not conversed with anyone?"

"Not a soul!"

"Well, the only two persons I have had dealing's with are Monsieur Rennecon and Monsieur Bompard, two well-established business men. I would trust Monsieur Rennecon to the hilt. I know he could not possibly be mixed up in that business. Therefore, it leaves just one other to suspect."

"Monsieur Bompard!"

"Exactly. I think, my lad, yes; I am quite sure, we shall have to keep a sharp weather eye on Monsieur Bompard."

CHAPTER 9. Sexton Blake's Suspicions of Monsieur Bompard Increase —But His Departure from Marseilles is Definitely Fixed.

WHATEVER suspicions may have been growing in Blake's mind regarding Bompard, that feeling did not cause him to suspend negotiations with the man. On the contrary. He had already inspected two ships which Bompard recommended, and had almost decided to charter one of them—a small eight-hundred tonner, which he thought would just about suit his purpose.

Forewarned was forearmed, and he made up his mind that he would go ahead just as he had intended, but, nevertheless, would watch the Provencal closely. The charter party rate was reasonable enough, Blake thought. The equivalent of a hundred shillings a ton, and that together with the necessary stores, and so on, could be handled for less than six thousand pounds.

That was one way. For the return voyage it had been tentatively agreed that, should Captain Beaumont run back in ballast, he would pay a return charter of fifty shillings; but if with cargo another hundred.

At that they had left it, so that Captain Beaumont could think it over during the evening, and, when he had finished with Bompard, Blake had gone on to see Monsieur Rennecon. That gentleman had spent a busy day and was all ready with a mass of figures for Blake's consideration.

Tin plate was selling on a strong market, but that didn't matter to Blake, so long as he could dispose of it at a profit in Odjiska. There again the commission agent proved useful to him, for he stated that he could make a firm offer by cable to a correspondent there, and perhaps arrange the sale before Blake cleared from Marseilles.

Blake was only too willing to agree to this, for he certainly was not hankering after the job of hawking several hundred tons of tin plate about Odjiska. So he left the whole thing in Rennecon's hands, after he had approved of the minimum quotation, c.i.f., which would see him through with a working profit.

Rennecon stated that he would of course offer at a higher figure than that, and if the market was bare at Odjiska, then Blake should make a very handsome thing out of it.

As to the fertiliser, he was even more optimistic. He was sure he could sell the whole cargo by cable at a good profit, and Blake was only too pleased to give him a chance to make the extra commission, so long as it relieved him of trouble.

When these details had been arranged, Blake broached the subject of the ship which he was thinking of chartering.

"She is a French craft, monsieur," he said in a casual tone, "and I think will do. I can't afford, with the capital at my command, to run with too much empty space. From the look of her engines I think she is going to be greedy on coal, but that can't be helped, and other economies may offset the extra expense. Monsieur Bompard is of the opinion that I shall be quite satisfied with her. He informs me that he has chartered her before, and has only heard words of praise for her."

Rennecon smiled.

"There isn't any man in Marseilles who knows more about chartering here than Bompard. But he is Provencal, monsieur, which means—" And he finished with an expressive shrug.

"He seems anxious enough to please," went on Blake.

"With Bompard, business is business, monsieur. No doubt he will do all he can. It is to his advantage."

"I have been wondering if I should leave all the stores and bunkering and hiring of the crew to him. He has offered to relieve me of the responsibility."

"Then I should do so. He will get his whack out of it, but he will be as fair as anyone else."

"There is one item on which I am always very particular, Monsieur Rennecon. I am wondering if you could help me out in it."

"If it is in my power, then with pleasure, monsieur."

"I have always been very particular about the sort of ship's carpenter I carry. It is some time since I have been in this port, and I do not know where to find the type of man I want. I wonder if you could, without bothering Bompard, find me a man whom I can trust entirely. I want a man who will be entirely the captain's man and nothing else."

Monsieur Rennecon rubbed his chin thoughtfully. Then suddenly his face lit up.

"Hein, monsieur, I know the very man for you. He is working in our own warehouse. He used to go to sea, but he has been ashore since the war. If he is willing to go I shall lend him to you. He is absolutely trustworthy."

"A thousand thanks, monsieur. When could I see him?"

"Any time—now if you wish."

"No! I will not trouble him while he is at his work. But, perhaps you could send him to my lodgings this evening?"

"Of a certainty. What time would be most convenient to you, M. le capitaine?"

"Shall we say between seven and eight?"

"It shall be done."

Shortly after Blake took his departure, to arrive at his lodgings with the result already known. That evening the carpenter turned up. One glance told Blake that the follow was one to be thoroughly depended on, a sturdy, frank-faced individual, who informed him that he came originally from Brest.

Blake warmed his heart in the way he talked of Brittany, and when he finally dismissed him it was agreed that, with Monsieur Rennecon's permission, he would sail to Odjiska and back as ship's carpenter. And, in a casual way, Blake impressed upon him that he was not to talk of the business among his comrades.

That evening he and Tinker had dinner at the Rotonde and turned in early. The next morning Tinker was left on guard at the house while Blake went off to see Bompard. He found that individual in his office, and informed him immediately that he had decided to close with the charter for the Germaine, the name of the small tramp which had been under discussion.

He then produced his letter of credit from Paris—he had taken good care to have it made out to Captain Alphonse Beaumont—together with two letters of recommendation from large shipping houses in Paris, which had been secured for him by M. Dupuis. When he read these, Bompard began to feel a little uneasy. He was wishing he had not been quite so precipitate in giving the hint to the Russian, for he should have been sorry indeed to antagonise either of those powerful firms and, judging by the tone of their letters, Captain Beaumont must stand ace high with them.

However, he consoled himself with the thought that, even if anything did happen, nothing could be traced to him, so he proceeded with the business as if he would rather cut off his hand than betray a client.

It took some hours to settle all the details about stores, coal bunkering and the like; and, finally, it came to the question of crew.

"I take it there is already a crew of some sort on board,"

remarked Blake.

"Yes, monsieur. But you will need half a dozen extra hands, and two more for the engine-room. I can undertake to arrange that for you if you wish."

"If you will be so good," returned Blake carelessly. "What about my officers?"

"There is a mate, but no second. The engineer will also go with you. I can send a second to you, if you wish."

"We will leave that until I go aboard; then you might do so, please."

"You will go on board at once?"

"To-morrow, if things are ready. I'd rather live aboard than ashore, and, besides, I want to be there to see after the stowing of the cargo. If I knew my mate I would not bother; but with a strange first officer I shall keep an eye on things."

"You will find him a competent man, I believe. The former captain spoke very highly of him. In fact, the Germaine would not be for charter, only that the former captain died suddenly, and the owners are in rather a bad way just now."

"Well, they will make a profit out of this charter, even if it isn't much. I take it you will arrange about that draft immediately, and let me have the final charter papers for signing as soon as possible."

"Not later than to-morrow morning, monsieur."

"That will do, and afterwards I shall go aboard."

With that Blake went on to see Rennecon, and, as he walked along, he was frowning so heavily that two small boys gave him the whole pavement to himself. He was pondering on Bompard.

"I'm hanged if I can figure him out!" he was thinking. "He seems straight and above board enough. But you never can tell—with a Provencal."

He dismissed these thoughts, however, as soon as he entered Monsieur Rennecon's office, for he found the commission agent feeling decidedly well pleased with himself, he had received replies to both of his cables, and in each case his firm offer had been accepted without any counter offer coming back. The only fly in the ointment, as far as M. Rennecon was concerned, was that he hadn't quoted a higher price for the tin plate.

But, when he figured out the margin of profit, Blake was more than satisfied. As a business proposition, he stood to make a pretty good thing out of his impromptu voyage, even if he never laid eyes on the gold bullion.

He gave the commission agent carte blanche to arrange about the purchase of the cargo, and informed him that he had closed matters with Bompard.

"I shall ask him to advise you at what dock he will berth the Germaine," he added.

But Rennecon waved his hand.

"Leave that to me, monsieur. I shall go and see Bompard this afternoon, and fix up all the details. If convenient, you might drop in and see me to-morrow. There will be some purchase contracts to sign."

Blake left it at that, and until the following day he and Tinker idled away the time. Just before midday Blake saw Bompard again, and completed the charter party papers; and, afterwards, he signed the purchase contracts with Rennecon. Bompard informed him that the Germaine would berth at his own wharf, in the old basin, and took him along to point it out.

"She will warp in this afternoon, monsieur, and you can go aboard to-night. If you will come to my office late in the afternoon I shall take you aboard and introduce your first officer to you."

Thus, on the surface, things went as smoothly as possible. In due course the flat, heavy crates of tin plate were stowed away, and on top of them the bagged fertiliser. The balance of the crew was secured and the two extra men for the engine-room.

And finally, on the day before everything was ready for clearing, Bompard brought aboard a second mate.

He was a forbidding-looking rascal, so both Blake and Tinker thought, and as he surveyed him Blake was thinking that he would have done better to pick one himself. He would have been much more strongly of that opinion if he had guessed for a single moment that the man in question had been supplied to Bompard by a certain Cheka agent with whom Bompard had secret and sinister dealings.

But Blake knew nothing of that, and he was still uncertain whether Bompard had been double-dealing or not when, five days later, he stood on his own bridge while the pilot conned them out of the harbour, and his last view of Bompard's wharf showed Bompard and Monsieur Rennecon waving good-bye.

"One of the pair has played me false—I am sure of it," Blake muttered to Tinker when the two were alone for a moment. "I am dead certain Rennecon is as straight as a die; so it must be Bompard. But how has he done it? That is what I can't figure out."

He was to learn before many days had passed.

CHAPTER 10.   Monsieur Bompard Makes Another Proposition to the Agent of the Cheka—Rymer's Voyage and Reception at Odjiska.

AS for Monsieur Bompard, that astute gentleman had enjoyed a decidedly strenuous time between his newest clients. Although they were each after the same thing they needed vastly different treatment; and, even at that, Bompard was not so sure that they were not bound up on the same business.

It was a strange coincidence that ships, small tramps good for little else just then the way the charter market was, should be in urgent demand for the same Russian port. It became still stranger when one considered that one of his most lucrative clients of late was a Bolshevist who, while he did not wish to charter, was willing to pay big money for information about anyone who did.

What was the meaning of it all, Bompard asked himself again and again. The fact that the bearded man and his chic little companion had, in a way, come from Halloran, was sufficient to convince Bompard that their business, at least, would not bear too close a scrutiny from the authorities.

His Russian paymaster, too, seemed to attach a good deal of importance to the doings of the couple, to judge from the readiness with which he unloosened his roll of banknotes each time that Bompard had information to impart.

But the other—he was a somewhat different proposition. Not that he appeared to have any better grasp of what he needed for a charter than the bearded one. It wasn't anything of a technical sort. It was more the way in which each client stated his wants; and Monsieur Bompard was an old, old hand at studying the mannerisms of his clients.

Something was going on in the Crimea which had a considerable interest for these strangers. It was sufficient to cause Halloran, the shipchandler at Port Said, to take a hand, and Bompard knew better than to under-estimate that.

It was no "cinq sous" jaunt across the harbour to charter a ship, bunker her, fill her with stores and, above all, make cargo arrangements. All that took money hard cash payable on the nail, and with this commodity both his new clients seemed to be well supplied.

Even if Bompard had known what was the lure at Odjiska there would have been no danger of him becoming a competitor. That sort of thing was not Bompard's style. To learn the secret—yes; that was different. A secret can always be sold. It can be turned into cash, and so he would have given a good round sum himself to know just what it was that was taking two tramps into the Black Sea at a time when the freight markets there were in a most depressed condition.

Well, he figured, he had the Russian who was apparently still as full of money as of vodka. As long as he had a thousand francs left Bompard would feed him with information.

But before those two tramps cleared from Marseilles he (Bompard) must manage to make a big play if the mystery possessed the material to support one. He had a feeling that once the two tramps did get away from Marseilles he would never see them again, and in that he was right.

It was plain that beyond what he could stick on in the charter-party deals he had little chance of robbing his two new clients. But until those vessels did clear he had free access to them and he knew a trick or two. If the Bolshevist was so keen to know when they would be ready to clear, he might also be willing to pay a round sum to know what happened on board them after they departed; and it was on that which Bompard fiddled.

But it was before his newest client, Captain Beaumont, arrived on the scene that Bompard had come to the conclusion that he must do all in his power to squeeze Halloran protegé before the latter got away.

Mary Trent's instinct was true. Bompard would have been only too delighted to philander with such an attractive-looking woman; but no matter how far his gallantry might have been permitted it would have made no difference to his plans to "skin" Rymer to the fullest possible extent.

There was, of course, a certain danger to be anticipated from Halloran. The shipchandler was no infant, and Bompard knew exactly what Halloran would do to him it he suspected that he had betrayed him.

But the Provencal did not intend that Halloran should know what was going on. There were lots of ways of covering up one's tracks and, after all, this man sent by Halloran was out on some illicit expedition or Bompard missed his guess very badly.

Port Said was a long way from Marseilles and, so far as he could see, Bompard would have no occasion to go to Port Said at any time. No; he figured himself quite sharp enough to diddle Rymer and Halloran both.

But one thing about Bompard was that he failed to allow for the quick mental process with which Mary Trent was equipped; and, further, he under-estimated Rymer—a fatal mistake. Not that this meant he was not going to be successful in his immediate plans, but Huxton Rymer was not the man to take a double-crossing lying down. A day of reckoning must come.

When he had seen things moving along in a way which promised an early departure of Rymer and Mary Trent from Marseilles, Bompard again sought out the evil-smelling Russian who had proved such a gold mine to him. He found him in his usual place, guzzling vodka at a rate which made delirium tremens a dead certainty before very long.

But what Bompard had to propose on this occasion was not to be spoken of in such a public place, and with some difficulty he persuaded the Cheka agent to come along with him to his office.

"Well, what is it this time?" demanded the Russian when they were in Bompard's private bureau.

"Things progress, monsieur," purred Bompard. "I have further news for you which I shall tell you without the usual— formality."

"Curses and hades! So I am to get something for nothing, am I? It can't be worth much if you give it away."

Bompard would have quite cheerfully stuck a knife into the fellow's gizzard for his insolence; but he would swallow almost any insult if gold lay beyond, as what Provencal won't.

"One does not always communicate news for the purpose of material gain," he said sententiously. "Things move, monsieur. The ship leaves in a few days at the outside."

"Those people?"

"Yes. The others will be a little longer. But we shall speak of them when the time comes. I have a proposal to make, monsieur."

"Curses and hades! I thought so. That means more money."

Bompard shrugged.

"That is entirely with you, monsieur. And I would remind you that had it not been for me you would have known nothing—nothing of all this. Is that not so?"

"By the holy ikon in which I don't believe, but you have been well paid," leered the Russian. "But come on, you fat robber—what have you to suggest?"

"I have not asked what it is that makes these people so anxious to go to the Crimea," went on Bompard slowly. "Nor do I intend to ask—"

"Curses and hades! You speak wisely. If you knew it would be a bad thing for you, robber!"

"I don't want to know," interrupted Bompard. "It is enough for me that I do my legitimate business. But it must be possible that their movements are of great interest to you, or you wouldn't pay so much. I, too, hear news from London, monsieur. There have been bad doings there; there were certain things here. Need I say more? Or shall I add that we are in Marseilles; Marseilles is in France—not in Russia."

The Bolshevist's piggy eyes grew wary. He might bluster and curse and heap insults upon the Frenchman's head, but he knew that the Provencal was a very slick crook all the same, and if it came to a game of finesse Bompard was a man to be reckoned with.

There was just the hint of the claw beneath the soft pad of that voice, and it penetrated through the drink-sodden mind of the Russian more surely than any blustering would have reached him.

"You keep your tongue between your teeth!" he snarled. But the words had no bite, as Bompard was quick to notice. "What is it you have to propose?"

"I have been thinking that if these people go to Odjiska on business which touches your affairs, monsieur, it would not be a bad plan if they remained there."

"Curses and hades! That is a suggestion. What do you mean?"

"Let us say, monsieur, that there is something there which is worth bringing away. If they remain there they fail, do they not?"

"They! What 'they' do you mean?"

"The first two who came to me for a ship."

"The man and the woman?"

"Yes."

"We know how to deal with people like that in Russia. But if they did not come back what about the ship?"

"I have a plan, monsieur; it is a scheme which has needed a great deal of thinking out. I am willing to tell you what it is, and to arrange everything so it cannot fail, if you will pay my price. But before one sou passes between us I am prepared to give you the outline gratis. If you like it, I elaborate; if you do not like it you pay me nothing. Is that fair?"

"It sounds all right; but you'll get more money, never fear. Where you are, you fat robber, money flies. But go on."

"You say if those people remained in Russia they could be dealt with safely?"

"Curses and hades! Of course! Once they are in Russian territory it is easy. They can be arrested for spying; and once in one of our gaols they stay there, my friend."

"Good. In this case the longer the better. The rest is easy. They have chartered a ship from me. I have made out charter-party papers in the matter. That is all in order. Now I make out a second set of charter-party papers to you or to someone whom you may nominate. These papers I know how to arrange so that they will appear all in order. Very well. When the ship gets to Odjiska your authorities there take care of these people as arranged. Their papers are confiscated, and you or your agents take over the ship. You are provided with a perfectly genuine set of papers, and with the stamping of your own authorities the whole thing becomes regular. In that way the two persons of whom we speak disappear into your gaols; you do as you wish with the ship to the end of the charter term. It would be wise to bring an ordinary cargo back to Marseilles. After that the charter finishes. You turn over the ship and the business is ended. Does that appeal to you, monsieur?"

"Curses and hades! It is the thought of a genius, fat robber! For how much will you do this?"

Thus did Monsieur Bompard consummate a fresh deal. It promised all in all to be a good season for that gentleman.

If Huxton Rymer had taken more to heart the warning Mary Trent had given him, Bompard might not have found it quite so easy to push his treachery so far. But Rymer, as always, was just a little too confident of his own abilities to handle any situation which might arise.

The result was that when he did get away from Marseilles, he had on board—but without his knowledge—a hand whose purpose there was well understood by Bompard and the Cheka agent.

Even then, if Rymer had had any suspicions of Bompard other than that he was a wily rascal, and would diddle him if he could, they would have been dulled as the voyage proceeded, for no mariner could have asked for a better run than he had down the Mediterranean.

They made the Bosphorus without incident, logging up the knots at a rate that, considering the sort of tub they were in, was satisfactory enough. Even Mary threw aside her cautiousness when they slid into the Black Sea and headed north towards Odjiska.

Everything seemed to be going without a hitch, and there seemed nothing to worry about until they should come up against the concerte problem which awaited them at Odjiska.

But there the blow fell.

It was late afternoon when they cast anchor in Odjiska Harbour. Little did either Rymer or Mary Trent dream, as the chain rattled out that had it not been for other treachery of Bompard's a second ship might have reached that anchorage ahead of them.

It was curious, in a way, that, considering Bompard's close association with both Rymer and Blake, neither of the old foes had known of the other's presence; but, of course, even if Rymer had passed Blake he would scarcely have recognised him in his disguise.

The anchor was no more than down when a launch put off from the shore. Thinking it would contain harbour officials coming to examine his papers, Rymer had a ladder thrown down, and stood at the top of it waiting to receive them.

Three men came up, each wearing some fragment of a uniform. On stepping on deck one after the other gave Rymer a close scrutiny, but it was not until the last was frowning upon him that the adventurer began to suspect that something had gone wrong. It was this last individual who did the speaking.

"You are in command of this ship?" he asked curtly in French.

Rymer acknowledged that to be the case.

"I will see your papers. I wish to be taken to your chart-room."

Rymer felt more inclined to heave him over the side, which would have been easy enough; but he knew those sort of tactics would not go in this place, so, with a polite gesture; he led the way to the bridge.

There they encountered a young man, who gave a quick glance at Rymer as he passed, and the slightest flicker of an eyelid on Rymer's part was a warning that things did not look too good. The young man was subjected to a stare on the part of all three Bolshevists, but not one suspected then that the "young man" was in reality a girl. It had been thought wise for Mary to masquerade in this fashion, and it might have proved worth while had there not been a traitor on board.

But neither she nor Rymer knew anything of the cable that had been sent to Odjiska warning the Cheka agents of their coming, nor did they know of the spy who had sailed with them.

In the chart-room Rymer submitted his papers. The senior of the trio professed to make a careful study of them; then he went through the manifests. At the end of that he suddenly demanded a list of the crew.

Rymer dug it up and passed it over. This time all three officials gave it their attention, talking together in low tones, and finally the spokesman swung round.

"I shall want the crew lined up on deck for inspection by the doctor," he said sharply. "See that not one is missing!"

"Very well. I shall see to it at once."

Leaving the chart-room, Rymer swung himself down to the deck and got hold of the bo'swain. In a few seconds the whistle was shrilling, and, as the men appeared, Rymer got them into line.

While he did so, the three Bolshevists stood on the bridge watching him, and, at a signal from Rymer that all his crew was mustered, two of them descended.

He who was, presumably the doctor, began at the end of the line and went slowly along. Had Huxton Rymer not been one of the finest surgeons out of Europe, he might not have seen that the whole thing was a farce. But being what he was, he soon spotted that the examination was being staged solely for some other purpose, and presently he saw what was afoot, although he could not fathom the reason.

In the middle of the line was a man who had been among those supplied by Bompard. Rymer had taken no particular notice of the fellow on the way, but his keen eye would have been quick to detect any signs of disease in any of the crew. Therefore he was amazed when the Cheka doctor motioned the fellow out of the line.

Taking him to the rail, he put a hand under his chin and tilted up his head, obviously examining his eyes. Rymer, extremely curious about the whole proceeding, approached, and, when the Russian had taken his hand away, said:

"What is it, monsieur? Are you under the impression the man has a disease?

"Not under an impression, monsieur—I know! How could you ship such a hand. He is suffering from tracoma! Look at his eyes!"

Rymer had already done so when he saw the other staring into them; but, as a matter of form, he caught the man under the chill and twisted his head round to the light. The eyes were as clear and healthy as his own. There was not the faintest trace of tracoma, and, no matter how stupid the Cheka doctor might be, he could not make any such mistake. It was bluff. But why?"

That was what Rymer was asking himself as he turned round. He was as wary now as a cat. Something was going on which he couldn't quite get the hang of. This statement that one of his hands was suffering from tracoma was sheer nonsense. Then why?

Was it part of a scheme to place them under quarantine and keep him stalled in the harbour for an indefinite time? If so, then what was the reason?

Could there be any suspicion against him? If so, how had it arisen? As far as he could see there had been no chance of betrayal, and yet—

"Yes, monsieur." he heard the Russian saying, "the man is suffering from tracoma. I am surprised that you were allowed to clear from Marseilles with one in this condition. He must be sent ashore at once. Tracoma is a thing which we must guard against in the strictest way."

If Rymer had held his peace then he might have had time to realise that a web was being spun about him, and to figure out some means of countering it. But so amazed was he at the bland statement that the man was suffering from an eye disease which he—Rymer—knew to be impossible, caused him to flare up.

He did not realise, until too late, that it was exactly what the Russian was playing for.

"That man—tracoma!" he spluttered. "But, monsieur, I tell you it is not so. The man is as healthy as you. I insist that he is in sound health, and I cannot permit you to drag him ashore until I have had him examined by another qualified man."

It was still more unfortunate for Rymer that he laid stress on that word "qualified." The Russian was not very fluent in French, but he knew enough, and his quick ear caught the nuance of contempt which Rymer put into the word.

"So," he murmured, fixing Rymer with a jaundiced eye. "Are you a doctor, monsieur?"

The quick question caught Rymer unawares.

"I— Why, I am a master mariner," he said, saving, himself just in time.

"In that case you would have done better to attend to things with which you are acquainted. As for me, monsieur, I tell you this man is suffering from tracoma. He will have to be sent ashore at once. I shall recommend that the ship be placed under strick quarantine until I am satisfied that the rest of the crew have not incurred the same disease. As for you, monsieur, I shall feel it my duty to report that you have offered opposition to the representative of the port authorities. My colleagues will bear me witness. You will not leave your ship without permission. I think you may count on hearing further from the authorities to-night. Now, you," he added, turning to the man who had been under discussion, "get over the side and into the boat. You are going ashore."

Rymer took a step forward. For a moment that doctor was as close to being smashed to a pulp as ever in his life. But in the crisis of the moment, Mary Trent, who had been watching and listening from the bridge, coughed. Rymer paused and made a gesture.

"Very well, monsieur," he muttered. "Make whatever report you wish!"

With that he turned on his heel and remounted the bridge. He stood there until the three officials had departed in the launch; then he turned to Mary.

"I wish I had broken that shrimp's neck!" he snarled savagely. "Did you hear?"

She nodded.

"Yes; and saw. It would have done no good, old boy. There was a lot more in that than any question of the man's state of health. I was watching the other two, and I am sure certain signals passed between them and the seaman. I am beginning to think that there is a lot underneath all this, that we have missed. It looks to me as if that man was a spy on board—that the medical examination was all bluff, and that it was the means used to get him ashore before you could go, so that he could make a full report on us."

"By heavens, Mary, but I believe you have struck the truth. But who could have sold us?"

"Bompard, of course. I have mistrusted him all along, and I feel it in my deepest instinct that he has betrayed us."

"Then that puts the lid on bringing off anything here!" remarked the adventurer gloomily. "If they are out for trouble we shall be lucky to get away with our skins. I don't like the look of things at all, Mary. I don't want to make you nervous, but I don't mind confessing that if I knew for a certainty that they were up to some devilry ashore I'd slip my anchor and run for it to-night. And if Bompard has betrayed us, then Heaven help him when I get my hands on him!"

"I don't see that we can do anything but stick tight," she said, gazing thoughtfully towards the shore. "If they are up to mischief then they will do something soon. If so, we may be able to get away, despite them. On the other hand, I don't think we ought to run unless we are sure. If that gold is so near to us I'd like to have one shot, anyway, at trying to get it."

"You are a brave girl, Mary, and the best partner a man ever had. We'll sit tight, as you say, and see what the night brings. I have a feeling that dirty little rat will spring something nasty before many hours have passed."

And Rymer was right. It was something a lot nastier than he had bargained for. Nothing happened until after the evening meal. He and Mary were on the bridge, talking in low tones, when their attention was attracted by the sound of a regular 'chug-chug-chugging' coming across the harbour.

It came nearer and nearer, and it wasn't long before they caught sight of a good-sized launch bearing down upon them.

"Here comes trouble, Mary," muttered Rymer, as he watched it. "If something breaks, my dear, you keep out of it, I shall not do anything foolish, but these birds are up to mischief all right. If they do get the better of me—well, little one, you'll have to do as you think best. But mind! Keep out of this."

With that, Rymer swung down the ladder to the deck and reached the side just as the first of a gang of men began to come aboard.

Remembering his promise to Mary, he tried to speak civilly, demanding what the invasion meant, but in response one of the gang jerked out a paper, read something from it in Russian, and then, almost before Rymer knew what was intended, they were upon him.

He put up a great fight. From the moment his fist crashed into the jaw of the one who had done the reading of the warrant, he went berserk. Man after man went down, and to the anxious Mary it looked for a time as if, even at odds of twenty to one, Rymer would drive them back over the side.

He might have done so, and he certainly would have succeeded, if he had had a chance to use his gun. But they had rushed him too quickly for that, and it was when five of them piled in at him together, that a sixth grabbed up a belaying-pin and brought it down with terrific force on the back of Rymer's head.

He staggered for a moment, and, lifting his head, tried frantically to say something to Mary. Then he dropped like a log.

CHAPTER 11.   Sexton Blake's Sensational Voyage to Odjiska.

BLAKE had made no attempt to speak privately to the ships carpenter before sailing, nor did he do so until they had passed down between Sardinia and Corsica, and had rounded the toe of Italy. But then one day, as they were dipping into the teeth of the stiff easterly breeze, he descended from the bridge and walked forward to where the man was at work, he watched him in silence for a few moments, then:

"I want you to come to my cabin this evening," he said briefly. "Come at nine o'clock."

The carpenter turned up at the hour named, and, behind a closed door, Blake conversed with him for the better part of half an hour. At the end of that time the matter which he had wished to arrange had been settled, and now the first part of his plan depended entirely upon the carpenter.

What Blake wanted done was something that could not be done openly. On the contrary. It was a matter requiring the greatest secrecy, and for that reason alone would have to be spread over a considerable period of time; but, with two weeks or more ahead of them before they could possibly make Odjiska, Blake figured that with luck the job could be done, and it is indicative of the secrecy with which he was working that not even Tinker knew what was afoot.

On the third day out they saw in the distance an Orient boat homeward bound. If Blake had dreamed for a single moment that Huxton Rymer and Mary Trent were on that boat he would have been perplexed.

Knowing Rymer as he did he would have known that the adventurer would not make a trip to Port Said and return in the month of August for mere pleasure, and perhaps he would have been more suspicious than he was back in Marseilles; but he knew nothing of their presence so close to him, and that same night he had other matters to occupy his mind.

He had been on the bridge most of the day, for what had been now only a stiff breeze was working up into a gale. After the evening meal he retired to his cabin, quite a roomy affair for that type of ship, and was busy going over ship's accounts when Tinker, who since leaving Marseilles had been acting as his personal attendant, entered.

"I have just come from the bridge, sir. The chief officer asked if you can come up for a few minutes. He has something to say to you."

Blake rose at once, and climbed the short companion to the bridge, for his cabin was situated almost beneath it. On seeing him the chief officer left the man at the wheel and came to meet him.

"I have a report to make, sir," he said.

"Yes," inquired Blake, "what is it?"

"Shortly after relieving the second this evening I had occasion to return to my cabin for something I had forgotten. On my return I saw the second in conversation with one of my stokers. I feel it my duty to tell you, sir, that they seemed to be conversing in a manner unfitting between an officer and an engine-room hand."

Blake regarded the man steadily. Since leaving Marseilles he had studied both his officers as well as the engineer with the greatest care, and he had already satisfied himself that the chief was not only a good seaman, but a thoroughly dependable man —a typical mate who would stick to his captain to the last ditch.

The engineer was purely nondescript, but he had to confess that the antipathy he had felt towards the second mate had increased. To begin with, the man was slovenly in his work, and secondly, had the habits and manners of a hedgehog. Had his papers not been in perfect order it would have been difficult for Blake to believe that he had ever passed his examination.

He had more than once regretted leaving the choice of a second to the last moment, for then it had been too late to pick another.

He voiced nothing of this, however, to the chief, merely thanking him and telling him that he would look into the matter. He did not return direct to his cabin, but descended to the main deck and walked aft. As he passed the open iron doorway which led down into the engine-room he saw a figure emerge, and drew up with a frown as, in the gloom, he recognised the second mate. He accosted the man.

"Monsieur, it is not customary, I believe, for a deck officer to intrude in the engine-room."

"I go to see the engineer," came the reply, in a distinctly surly tone.

"In future when you wish to speak to the engineer you will do so on deck or in the saloon." snapped Blake.

The man mumbled some reply, and moved on, while Blake continued his way round the deck. It was by pure chance that, as he passed the skylight over the saloon, he paused to look down. As he did so he saw Tinker pass through, and then, at an angle of vision, he caught sight of someone seated at the table. It was the engineer.

He returned in a thoughtful mood to his cabin, on the upper deck. Sitting on the side of his bunk, he lit a cigarette and rang for Tinker. When the lad appeared he motioned to him to close the door.

"Do you know how long the engineer has been in the saloon?" he asked, in a low tone.

"Not exactly, guv'nor—twenty minutes or so, I should think."

"Do you think there is any chance that the second mate knew he was there?"

"I don't know, sir; but he has been mouching about the deck for some time."

"All right, young 'un, you might keep your eye on him without making it too obvious."

"What's up, guv'nor?" whispered Tinker.

"Perhaps nothing, but I am a little puzzled over something."

And when Tinker was gone Blake regarded the two incidents in their relation to time.

"It is about half an hour since he was relieved by the first mate," he muttered. "He knows perfectly well what time the engineer comes up for his supper. First, however, he has a talk with one of the stokers, which is conducted in such a way as to win the disapproval of the chief officer. Following that he descends into the stokehold, and, on being challenged by me, informs me that he has gone down to see the engineer. Now, did he mean to imply, or, rather, did he want me to understand that he had gone down to see the engineer not knowing he was on deck, or did he intend to convey that he had actually seen him? I cannot but believe that he knew the engineer was in the saloon, and, that being so, what was he doing in the engine-room in his absence? I'll keep an eye on that surly brute. He'll bear watching, or I miss my guess."

But the mischief was done, and shortly after midnight Blake knew it. He had been lying awake with the light on, and was gazing up at the tell-tale compass overhead when suddenly the whole ship seemed to quiver, and then came the sudden cessation of the throb of the propeller.

Blake was on his feet like a flash, and not stopping to put on his shoes dashed out of the cabin. Just as he reached the deck he met the first mate, who had also been roused—he had been relieved a short time before by the second—and questioned him.

"I don't know, sir—I think it is the engines."

"Go up on the bridge and take charge," ordered Blake. "I will go to the engine-room."

On the main deck he met Tinker.

"Come on," he said, as he ran along. "Something wrong in the engine-room."

They went down, or, rather, slid down the iron ladders which led into the bowels of the ship; but scarcely had they reached the bottom when they met the engineer and the four stokers scrambling to climb up, the next second Blake saw the reason, for there came a loud hissing noise as two safety cocks opened and steam began pouring out.

Blake knew it was useless to attempt to do anything until the blow-off should end, so he motioned to Tinker to go back, and up they went one after the other, like so many ants crawling from a hole.

On deck Blake turned to the engineer.

"What is wrong?" he asked, curtly.

The engineer, who was in a state of great excitement, spread out his hands tragically.

"I do not know, sir," he cried. "Something has gone wrong with my engines— with my dear, good engines which have never before given me trouble. It is that a shaft has buckled, or packing has blown out. When the blow-off finish I go to see."

Whatever it was that had caused the trouble Blake knew that the little engineer was perfectly sincere. His concern was too genuine for him to be doubted, and then Blake thought of the report which the first mate had made to him, and of the lie which the second had told him. His mind worked swiftly as he regarded the four stokers, then he turned to Tinker.

"My compliments to the chief officer, and ask him if he will come here," he said curtly

Tinker raced up the companion to the bridge, and a few moments later the first mate came tumbling down the ladder.

"Of these four men which one was in conversation with the second mate?" asked Blake.

Unhesitatingly the chief pointed to the second man from the left—one Blake knew that had been taken on at Marseilles.

"Stand out, you!" he ordered. "And you, too!" he added, pointing to the second man who had been supplied by Bompard.

Blake was in an ugly mood. It was perfectly clear to him now that the second mate was behind the accident—accident by design—in the engine-room. There could be no doubt now that Bompard had double-crossed him, and he blamed himself for not having dealt with that phase of it in Marseilles.

But he had counted on things being completely under his control once he got to sea, and because he was so anxious to preserve the secrecy of his own identity that he had let the matter pass.

He had no means of knowing how many of the crew may have been tampered with since leaving port, but he did know that now was the time for a show down and a test of strength, so he played his hand.

"Someone has tampered with the engine," he said harshly. "It is one or both of you. You are going to have one chance to confess."

But both men were silent, and Blake wasted no further time.

"Monsieur," he said, turning to the first mate and pulling out his revolver as he spoke, "you will take four men to the bridge and arrest the second mate. You will take him, please, to the saloon for the time being and keep him under guard. Then return here with four more men and put this pair in irons. If there is any disinclination on the part of the crew to obey orders, let me know at once."

"Bien, monsieur!"

When the chief had departed, the little engineer made as if he would speak, but Blake waved him to silence.

"Wait," was all he said.

Five minutes or so passed, and then the measured tramp of feet came along the deck as the second mate, guarded by four sailors, was brought along, followed by the chief with drawn revolver.

They disappeared down the companion leading to the saloon, and presently the first mate reappeared. They saw him go forward, but he was back in less than no time, accompanied by four more men, two of whom carried irons.

There was no politeness wasted over the job. The irons were clamped on without ceremony, and the two stokers dragged away to be locked in the lazaret.

"Who is in charge on the bridge?" inquired Blake, when the first mate returned to report that orders had been carried out.

"The quartermaster, sir."

"He can carry on for the time being. I want you in the saloon, please."

But if Blake had expected to get anything out of the second mate he was disappointed, for the man maintained a stubborn silence to all his questioning. Blake gave it up.

"Put him in irons," he ordered curtly, "and lock him in his cabin."

It was then that the fellow broke into sudden violence, but in a sudden gust of rage Blake sprang forward and levelled him with a single blow.

"The quartermaster will act as second mate," said Blake when the chief had rejoined him in the saloon.

"Very good, sir."

"Does the rest of the crew seem all right?"

"Yes, sir, there was no hesitation to obey orders."

"You can depend on the quartermaster?"

"Absolutely, sir. He has sailed with me for some time."

"Very good, I shall take the bridge myself presently, and I need not add that I am extremely obliged for the promptitude with which you reported matters to-night."

Five days they rolled about in the Mediterranean while the engineer struggled with his engines. Five precious days were lost, and if Blake had known that another ship was even then leaving Marseilles on the same mission, he would have fumed still more, but there was no help for it.

He knew the engineer was doing his best, and on the sixth day came the welcome announcement that the engines would start.

"Give them all they will stand," was his order, and from that day on, the ancient tramp wallowed eastward up through the Dardanelles and into the Black Sea at a rate which she had not achieved since her maiden trials.

It was on a chill September morning that they at last cast anchor in the harbour of Odjiska. Not a biscuit toss away was another tramp, somewhat larger than the Germaine, but uglier in her lines. She, too, was flying the French flag, but Blake had no idea that it was this craft which had left Marseilles while they wallowed helplessly off the entrance to the Adriatic. Ugly though she was, she had had the speed of them, and two nights before had passed them, although she had been too far away for them to sight her.

Half the morning was consumed over port formalities. It was then that Blake realised to the full just what Count Torsky had meant when he said the Soviet agents were fine-tooth combing every craft that entered or cleared from Russian Black Sea ports, they studied his ship's papers as if they had never seen such documents before. The whole crew was lined up on deck, and each man inspected individually.

And then came the discovery that the second mate and two of the stokers were under arrest and in irons. Blake was questioned closely on this point, but he knew the law of the sea, and he knew his rights as commander of the ship.

He curtly informed them that it was a matter of conspiracy and insubordination. He knew exactly the risk he was running, but there was nothing to do but face it. He had sufficient proof to tell him that the second mate was in the pay of the Cheka, and he knew that it would be practically impossible to prevent the mate from signalling some sort of message to the Soviet official.

He was gambling on one thing only. If the second mate was a Russian, then things would become decidedly complicated, but, on the other hand, if he were a French Communist, who had been employed by the Cheka agents in Marseilles, then Blake might be able to bluff it through.

And he was inclined to believe the latter, for the man spoke French with the typical slur of the Provencal, and it was not reasonable to suppose that one of his low order of intelligence could have acquired such fluency, except he had come to France as a child. Later events proved that he was right.

There was no doubt that the Soviet officials were dissatisfied, but there was nothing they could do, except to leave two men on board to scrutinise every item of cargo which was sent ashore and to give orders forbidding all but the captain to go ashore.

Before departing they descended into the hold and inspected the cargo, but not even they could turn over several hundred bags of fertiliser, much less a few hundred tons of tin plate. That scrutiny would have to be left until the cargo was lowered into lighters.

When they were gone, Blake went to his cabin, closing and locking the door. Then seating himself on the edge of his bunk, he proceeded to do a very curious thing. Removing from his left foot one of the rubber-soled shoes he was wearing, he took out a heavy clasp-knife, and, using the largest blade, proceeded with the utmost care to separate the outer sole from the inner. Beginning at the toe, he prised it off bit by bit until more than half of it had been freed.

It might have been seen then that the rubber cement had only been applied for a quarter of inch or so in from the edge, and that the rest of the space had been utilised for the concealment of a folded piece of paper.

Removing this, Blake placed it beside him for the time being, then, opening his locker, he got out a small tube of quick-drying cement. He spread this inside the sole and pressed it back into place, after which he put it aside to dry. That done, he seated himself at the small writing flap which was just beneath the porthole, and wrote steadily for some minutes.

When he had finished, he folded the sheet of paper carefully, and with the other, which he had taken from between the rubber-sole, placed them under his left foot, inside the sock. He then put on his shoe again, and was in the act of gathering together the necessary documents to be handed to his consignees, when there came a rapid tap, tap at the door.

He turned the key and found Tinker standing outside. The lad pushed his way in and closed the door.

"Guv'nor," he said in a low tone, "I have just had the glasses on that tramp that is lying anchored close to us. There is someone on the bridge that looks like a boy, but I'll eat my boots if it isn't Mary Trent."

Blake gazed at him blankly.

"Mary Trent."

"Yes, sir, I am sure of it."

"I'll have a look."

Blake made his way to the bridge, and, taking up the glasses which Tinker had been using, trained them on the other craft. The figure to which Tinker had referred certainly looked like a youth, but, as the head was turned slowly in his direction, Blake felt as positive as Tinker that it was none other than Mary Trent. And where was Mary Trent there was Rymer also.

Blake drew back so that she should not see him. For the moment he and Tinker were alone on the bridge.

"Rymer must be there or ashore." he murmured. "Keep an eye on that craft and see if Rymer appears. I'll figure out what is to be done when I have finished my business in the town."

Then he descended to the main deck, and, climbing over the

94

ladder which hung at the side, dropped into the boat which he had ordered to be kept in waiting for him. It was a shore boat, for none of his own men were permitted to leave the ship.

And as he drew away from the side of the dirty little tramp, Blake realised that he had cut his last thread with the outside world. He was indeed entering the jaws of the Black Tiger.

CHAPTER 12.   "Your disguise is good, Miss Trent!"

ON reaching the jetty Blake had no need to ask his way, for the simple reason that two Soviet agents fell in, one on either side of him. They were perfectly polite in asking if they could be of assistance, but Blake knew he was being kept under strict guard, and as he went along to the consignee who had purchased the tin-plate, he was wondering how on earth he was going to manage a particular bit of business which must be carried out.

However, there was nothing to do but to trust to luck, and when he arrived at the warehouse, which was his first destination, he noted with inward satisfaction that the two guards did not attempt to enter with him.

He found his consignee was a man in a considerable way of business. Blake had an idea that before the last revolution he had probably been of royalist tendencies, and surmised that, like so many others, he had found it advisable to change his principles. After all, self-preservation is the thing that counts most with the average person.

He spoke French fluently, and transacted his business with Blake in an entirely satisfactory manner.

The Bolshevists might hate England and all its doings, but if they want to buy from no matter what country, they have got to pay in sterling on London. This was a condition of a contract which Blake's consignee had made with Monsieur Rennecon, and everything was in order against the landing of the cargo.

When this business had been completed and details for the lightering of the cargo arranged, Blake was escorted by his two guards to the other consignee who was to receive the fertiliser.

His business there was despatched in quite as satisfactory a manner as at the other place, and this individual promised to act without delay in arranging for lighters for the bag cargo so that the tinplate could be reached.

On emerging into the street Blake found his two attendants waiting for him. Now came the real test. If he failed this time he could only make another attempt, and still another and another if necessary until he succeeded in his object. He had already ascertained that one of the men spoke French, and now addressing him, he said:

"I am informed by the gentleman I have just left that there is a ship chandlery near at hand. I wish to order some engine-room stores, and would be obliged it you would show me to this place."

"The name, monsieur?"

Blake gave it, and they proceeded. If it were suspected that the ship chandler was still at heart faithful to the Czarist cause, Blake knew that he would have little hope of even a single private moment with him.

He reasoned on the other hand that if he were suspect he would scarcely be at liberty, and when on arriving at the place, the guards still remained in the street he knew that Torsky's agent still managed in some miraculous way to keep clear of suspicion.

The ship chandlery was a long, low, gloomy building in utter confusion. It was no little feat to make ones way through, and it was not surprising that when half-way down Blake stumbled over a pile of cordage, and came a heavy cropper. Up till then he had not seen a soul, but as he thudded to the floor a tall, gaunt-looking individual hurried to his assistance. Swiftly Blake grasped his wrist.

"Are you Mr. X.?" he asked in an urgent, whisper.

"'Yes; I am he. Who are you, please."

Blake uttered one word: "Torsky."

Then grasping his left ankle he swiftly unlaced his shoe. Jerking it off he rolled down his sock and caught hold of the two folded pieces of paper. He thrust them into the other's hands.

"Quick. Conceal them. There are two guards outside."

Without waiting to see what the other did with the papers he drew up his sock and put on his shoe, tying it hurriedly, for he thought he heard a step at the door, and well was it for him that he had lost no time, for at that moment one of the guards came sauntering in, and might even then have become suspicious had be not followed Blake's example by coming a cropper over some cordage.

By the time he had recovered himself and moved closer to where Blake was sitting he was inclined, from his own experience, to believe that Blake's fall had also been genuine.

The ship chandler was playing up nobly, being greatly concerned and solicitous over Blake's ankle. Between them they assisted Blake to his feet, but continuing his play on the bluff, Blake limped painfully at each step.

He accepted the ship chandlers apologies somewhat grumpily, and then laid on the counter the list of engine-room stores which he required. That, at least, was genuine enough, for the patching of the engines in the Mediterranean had been only a makeshift job at best.

It was with a grim sense of humour that Blake gripped each of his guards by the shoulder and bore all his weight upon them while he limped his way back to the jetty. He had a suspicion that they were as glad to get rid of him as he was of them, and when he got back to the small boat, headed again for the Germaine, he breathed an inward sigh of relief. The whole thing now was on the lap of the gods.

On reaching his own deck, he turned immediately to address the senior of the two Soviet officials, who had been left on board.

"There is no objection, I presume, to my making a courtesy visit to the other French boat, which is lying close?"

The man hesitated.

"We have no instructions, regarding that, monsieur."

"Then I shall go. You will be good enough, please, to instruct the men in the boat to row me across."

The man looked as if he would like to refuse, but in the absence of definite instructions he could scarcely do so. After all, the Soviet was not at war with France.

Before he could make up his mind Blake had dropped back into the boat, and the two men at the oars, taking it for granted that everything was all right, pulled away at his command.

On reaching the other ship Blake sent up a hail for a rope-ladder to be dropped down. Then he went over the side, and blushing aside the two Soviet officials who were on duty there, he climbed the companion to the bridge.

There was no one to be seen there now, but when he had sent up a loud "Hallo!" the door of the chart room opened, and a slim, youthful figure emerged. Standing so close as this, one glance was sufficient to tell Blake that Tinker had been right. It was indeed Mary Trent. Blake bowed and maneuvered her back into the chart-room.

He spoke hurriedly, for he knew that at any moment one of the port officials might come to investigate, and when he did speak it was in plain English.

"Your disguise is good, Miss Trent, but not good enough. Where is Rymer?"

The girl gave a startled gasp and shrank back against the chart table.

"You—who are you?" she asked with difficulty.

"I'll have to trust you and tell you. There is no time to be lost. I am Sexton Blake."

Her startled gaze held his, and then, while she could not even then pierce his disguise, she knew that he spoke the truth.

"I know why you are here, and you are on a fool's errand." he went on. "But where is Rymer? If these people learn the truth he won't stand a chance, nor will you."

"He—he went ashore yesterday to see about some cargo, but he hasn't returned. I don't know what has become of him."

"Then they have got him," returned Blake curtly.

"You—you say you know why we are here. It is you who have betrayed him."

"How could I betray him when I only got into port this morning. Besides, no matter what he may have done in other places I don't betray my own countrymen, or countrywomen, to these wolves, if you will feel safer you may come over to my ship. I will do what I can."

But she shook her head.

"No," she returned miserably. "I'll stay here until he comes."

There was a sound of a footfall on the bridge, and bending forward swiftly Blake whispered earnestly.

"Keep your courage. I'll do everything possible."

Then straightening up he went on in casually polite tones just as the door opened:

"Monsieur. I shall be happy if you will present my compliments to Monsieur le Capitaine. I regret that he is absent. I shall call and pay my respects another time."

With that he turned and brushing past the Soviet official, who had been regarding them suspiciously, he returned to the main deck and swung over the side into the boat.

It took four days to shift the cargo of fertiliser into the lighters, and not a single bag was there that went over the side that was not probed and prodded from top to bottom, and from side to side by a horde of Soviet agents.

During this time Blake had made two visits ashore, and on neither occasion did he attempt to visit the ship chandler. His business was with his consignees, and by careful inquiry he managed to elicit a half admission that the captain of the other French craft had been incarcerated in prison—for what reason he could not discover. It was Bompard again, although only later did Blake discover that.

Several times he had allowed Mary Trent to see him looking through the glasses, and on each occasion she had shaken her head in a way which told him that Rymer was still absent. But this, of course, he knew.

During those days he made another discovery, which was that the consignee who had bought his consignment of tin-plate was a man of considerable influence in the local Soviet, and there Blake concentrated his efforts.

It took time and patience, and eventually a considerable sum of money. But at the end of ten days, when the last lighter of tin-plate went ashore, he went with it, and that same afternoon, as mysteriously as he had been arrested, was Rymer released. He was gaunt and ragged, and Blake, who accompanied him down to the jetty, knew that he must have had a decidedly rough passage.

"You haven't a hope in a million of lifting that bullion, Rymer," he said curtly; without any attempt to beat about the bush. "If you take my advice you will up anchor and clear out while the going is good. If you don't they'll grab you again as sure as little apples ever grew on trees. I am no philanthropist, and you are the last man in the world I should hold a brief for, but I have no desire to see that bunch of wolves eat you up. If you wish you can abandon your own ship and sail with me."

"I've got nothing to say now," returned Rymer, "but I have sense enough to know how much chance I would have stood if it hadn't been for you. I'll remember this, and one day I'll pay the debt, but I'll stick to my own ship."

"I am curious to know one thing," said Blake just before they parted. "Did you charter in Marseilles?"

"Yes."

"From Bompard?"

"Yes."

"Well, Bompard double-crossed you, as he double-crossed me. That was why they gathered you in as soon as you got here."

Rymer stopped dead in his tracks.

"Do you know that for a fact?"

"Absolutely."

Rymer's fists clenched.

"I'll eat that bird when I get back to Marseilles," he snarled. Then he dropped into the boat, nor did he look back once the whole way between the jetty and his own ship.

Blake had already made up his mind to sail in ballast. It took another day and a half to load in bags of sand in sufficient quantity, but on the second afternoon, with all his papers in order and a Soviet official still on board to remain with him until he was well out to sea, when he would transfer to a harbour tug that was keeping him company, he gave the chief officer instructions to up anchor.

He was standing with his hands in his pockets, fists clenched until the knuckles were white, could one but have seen them, for now had come the most critical moment of all. But outwardly he was serene enough as he watched the crew man the capstan and begin to wind up the anchor chain. Up it came slowly, ever so slowly, until the look-out called "She's atrip," or the equivalent of that in French.

Then suddenly there came a sharp snapping sound, followed by a hearty curse from the chief officer, who was standing forward.

"Anchor chains gone, sir," he called. "A broken link."

Sexton Blake was not a profane man, but he cursed whole-heartedly at this misfortune, and it was in French at that.

Not even the Soviet official could expect a ship to put to sea without an anchor, or, rather, with only a light spare anchor which would have no chance of holding in heavy weather. When he had exhausted his flow of language Blake, who had assiduously cultivated this particular port officer during the past few days, turned to him and said:

"I'd give five thousand gold roubles if I could find another anchor without being delayed. I am late now. Do you think you can be of any assistance to me, monsieur?"

Five thousand gold roubles was more than two years' pickings for that official, and while the Germaine was steaming slowly back to her former anchorage, his mind was working swiftly.

"Let me think, monsieur. The ship chandler is also a blacksmith. He deals in junk, and may have one. I shall, if you wish, inquire."

"I shall be greatly indebted to you. My papers have all been completed, and I do not wish to go ashore again."

"You can depend upon me, monsieur, to do all in my power." And the official was quite at ease in his mind in promising, for, spy as they would, they had discovered not a single suspicious circumstance about the Germaine or her captain. She had been emptied of her cargo, Soviet labourers had loaded her ballast. Nothing else had been taken aboard except ordinary food supplies. Besides, the other ship was the one that had been chiefly suspected.

Therefore, while the Germaine swung round and pulled at her one remaining anchor, the Soviet official hastened ashore. He was back inside two hours, his whole attitude one of complete satisfaction.

"Monsieur, I have been fortunate," he exclaimed. "Beneath a heap of junk in the yard of the ship chandler we have found an old anchor and chain, which will do admirably. He demands five hundred gold roubles."

"I will pay it," agreed Blake. "I would pay more in order to get away quickly, and you, monsieur, if you will come to my cabin, I shall express my gratitude by handing you five thousand gold roubles."

It was evening when a lighter came off from the shore bringing the anchor and chain which had been found amongst other junk in the ship chandler's yard.

To be in readiness Blake had had the engineer open up the end link of the other bit of chain which still remained wrapped round the winch, and in half an hour after the anchor had been hoisted up the job was done.

This time no hitch occurred, and, instead of accompanying him out to sea, the Soviet official bade him a warm good-bye and returned to the town on the lighter. Never had man left Soviet Russia less under suspicion than Captain Beaumont of the Germaine.

*   *   *   *

They were a good fifteen miles off shore, making a course direct for the Golden Horn, when Tinker sought Blake in his cabin. There was a troubled expression in the lad's eyes as he closed and locked the door.

"I say, guv'nor, are you really going to leave without that bullion, or do you figure on returning?"

Blake, who was sitting on the side of his bunk smoking a cigarette and dangling his legs in a care-free manner, smiled at the lad.

"Despite the good impression we have made we are not returning, young 'un."

"But the gold, guv'nor?"

"The gold is on board, my boy."

Tinker goggled at him.

"On board—how on earth can it on board, guv'nor?"

"I see I shall have to give you more training in your powers of observation, young 'un." Then his voice sank to a murmur. "That old junk anchor and anchor chain, my lad—there is your gold, two tons of it."

Tinker sank down in amazement

"Oh, my hat—my hat!" he gasped. "And I never guessed it! How did you work it, guv'nor?"

"The ship's carpenter, young 'un. It took time, but he began filing at that anchor chain immediately we left Marseilles. By the time we reached Odjiska the anchor would stand a moderate holding, but it wouldn't stand the strain of being hauled up. Rough weather might have been our undoing. However, our luck held, and that's that. Two tons you'll find it weighs, my lad—and all cast and painted by that faithful old fellow in Odjiska."

*   *   *   *   *

For the second time within a few weeks Dr. Huxton Rymer took his way along the water-front at Port Said. On this occasion, however, he did not start from the Continental Hotel.

He had come ashore in a small boat from one of the smaller tramps that lay out in the roadstead—the same craft, in fact, in which he had made his ill-fated voyage to Odjiska.

But his destination was the same. He came once more to the sign which bore the name of "D. Halloran, Ship Chandler," and there he turned in. The same half-naked, gigantic Nubian was there, and, as before, Rymer paid no attention to him.

He continued on through the heterogeneous collection of marine stores, pushed open the door leading to the room at the back and found the ship chandler seated at his desk. He was dressed exactly the same, his attitude was exactly similar— it might have been that Rymer had never been away from Port Said.

He glanced up as the adventurer entered and closed the door.

"Well?" he inquired casually.

"It is far from well," responded his visitor. "The whole thing has gone up in smoke."

"I guessed as much from your message. By the way, how did you send it?"

"Passed a craft equipped with wireless on the way down. Signalled the message to them, and asked them to put it through."

"I thought as much. So we backed a loser, did we? Let me have the yarn."

Briefly Rymer gave him a resume of his doings since he had left Marseilles for Odjiska, and of all that had happened there. At the end he waited for Halloran's comments. They were exceedingly profane to begin with, but it finally emerged from the stream of blue language that he was deeply interested in the eternal perdition of Monsieur Bompard.

"He's our meat," he wound up. "I shall never rest until I get my claws into the crooked little Provencal."

The shipchandler was sublimely oblivious of his and Rymer's standing.

"As far as that bird Sexton Blake is concerned, I'm willing to take what he handed to us. It was a case of dog eat dog, anyway, and he beat us to it. That's all. But if you are certain Bompard double-crossed us then there isn't anything too bad for him. If he thinks he is going to get away with that kind of a deal and my money as well he has another think coming to him. What have you to say?"

"You couldn't have it in for Bompard more than I have," grunted Rymer. "I came here first because I knew you would want to know as soon as possible what had happened. But now I am going to Marseilles, and heaven help that dirty little rat when I get my hands on him."

"You wait a minute. I've got something to say there. You are not to have it all your own way. I want a shot at him, too."

"You are welcome to what I leave. I tell you he double-crossed me in Marseilles and after I left there. If it hadn't been for him I'd have lifted that gold out of Odjiska. I'll wring his fat neck for him as soon as I get back to Marseilles."

"And I say you won't! Now listen! What good would that do? What sort of a revenge is a few minutes beating up of that dirty rat? None at all. Does it get our money back? Not a sou. I have a much better plan. How about, this?"

Halloran began to talk and Rymer listened. As the shipchandler proceeded, Rymer nodded his head from time to time approvingly. At, last:

"You've got it, Halloran! I'll do my part!"

"All right. The sooner you get started the better. You just bring that bird here and I'll show you."

And that same evening Rymer got away again for Marseilles. On arriving at that port, his first care was to complete all formalities with the port authorities so that he could clear before evening if necessary. Not until then did he go ashore, leaving Mary Trent on the ship.

He was fortunate enough to find Monsieur Bompard in his office, and at sight of the big, bearded adventurer, that person's heart missed quite half a dozen beats. Bompard was a physical coward of the worst sort, and the life he had led had not hardened him any. On the contrary. Up to that moment he had believed Rymer still safely in a Bolshevist gaol.

Captain Beaumont, who had chartered the other vessel, had not yet returned from the Black Sea, and even if he had it is very doubtful if he would have communicated to Bompard any news concerning Rymer.

Bompard had "sold" Rymer both coming and going, and when he saw that bearded, aggressive face thrust so close to him, he was certain that he was in for something that was going to hurt, and hurt badly. He was—but not just then.

To his amazement, and extreme relief Rymer greeted him quite pleasantly. Somehow the ship-broker managed to stammer:

"Ah! You are back again, captain! I trust you had a pleasant and successful voyage."

"Quite!" responded the adventurer. "In fact, monsieur, so well did everything go, that I think I shall extend my charter of the vessel."

Bompard was inwardly astounded. Extend the charter of the vessel! The voyage a success! What could it mean? Had his work had no effect? Had this big man before him fooled the authorities at Odjiska after all? Well, here he was in the flesh, so there must have been a hitch in the Cheka plans somewhere.

If that were so, then so much the better for him. He had all the money there had been to get out of the deal. The Cheka agent was no longer in Marseilles, and Bompard had taken good care that the French authorities had received certain information that would keep him out.

So it looked as if things had fallen his way more favourably than even he could have planned. Another charter meant further pickings.

He rubbed his hands together.

"I shall be most pleased to do further business with you, captain. Are you thinking of chartering for a long voyage?"

"It promises to be a long journey," answered Rymer; and Bompard could not know that it was a journey he was to take that was to be a long one. "There are, however, one or two changes I shall want made," went on Rymer. "They won't cost much and I am willing to pay for them. They will be necessary for better stowage of cargo."

"There will be no difficulty about that."

"I hoped not. All the same, I should like you to have a look at what I propose doing before I call in the surveyors. Would it be possible for you to come aboard?"

"Most assuredly, monsieur. When would you wish it?"

"Well, I don't want to lose any time. I thought you might find it possible to come along now."

"I can do so. If you will give me a few minutes I shall leave some instructions."

So it was that at the end of another twenty minutes or so Rymer and Bompard departed in a fiacre for the outer basin where Rymer's ship was moored.

Bompard found the other most affable as they drove along, and inwardly he was puzzling as to how he had succeeded in pulling off things successfully in Odjiska and wondering just what it was he had gone after.

He must, he reckoned, have made a very good thing out of it to return in such high good humour—which promised well for Bompard.

Rymer dismissed the fiacre at the dock and conducted his guest on board. On reaching the deck, he stated that the changes he had in mind could be better seen by going below, so the broker, quite unsuspecting any treachery, followed obediently.

Rymer led the way along a passage until he came to a door which bore signs of having been newly erected.

"I had this put up on the way back," he announced as he threw it open, revealing a small bare cabin. "Some persons would complain that the place was dark and small and uncomfortable, but you and I wouldn't think so, would we monsieur? Ha, ha!"

"Ha, ha, ha!" echoed Bompard flatly. "You will have your little joke, monsieur, is it then that you take a passenger?"

"That is it, monsieur; someone who may think of the accommodation what I have said. But I think it will suit, don't you?" And he poked Bompard slyly in the ribs.

Bompard, thinking that he was being let into a secret and finding it quite funny to think of some unwilling passenger occupying that bare hole, laughed again. It would be as well to fit into the humour of this client, he thought.

"Ha, ha, ha!" he chortled.

"Ha, ha, ha!" went Rymer.

And then—

Out went the big man's hand catching Bompard in a grip of steel. The Frenchman squirmed, and his face went grey as he peered into the other's blazing eyes,

"Ha, ha, ha!" snarled Rymer. "So you think the accommodation suitable, do you, Bompard. That is well, for you are going to be the unwilling passenger, you crooked, thieving rat. You thought you had got away nicely with double-crossing me didn't you? You got a bit of a shock when I walked into your office to-day. From all your figuring I ought still to be in that filthy prison in Odjiska. This cabin, if you wish to call it a cabin, was built for you, Bompard. And in this you travel."

"B-but, monsieur, I—I beg of you—I appeal you are joking, monsieur—"

Rymer laughed harshly.

"Joking am I? We'll see how much of a joke you think it is when you meet Halloran at Port Said."

Bompard went grey, and his limbs became jelly.

Port Said—Halloran—this bearded devil who held him—

Fool that he was not to have suspected some devilry; why had he walked so blindly into this terrible trap—it could not be he would plead—he would offer money.

He did. He made of himself such a grovelling thing that Rymer sickened. When he could stand it no longer, he shut off the stream by twisting the collar of Bompard's coat until his face went purple. Then he hurled him bodily into one corner.

"If you kick up a row I'll give you something to remember the whole way to Port Said," he snarled. With that he stalked out and closing the door, locked it.

Some days later when the tramp was once more back in Port Said, it was Halloran who came to see Rymer instead of the later going ashore. Together they went down to Bompard, who was a poor shadow of what he had been before leaving Marseilles.

At sight of Halloran he began to whimper. He had been devilled by Rymer the whole way down the Mediterranean, and now he thought he was to be thrown to the mercy of this other, of whom he had heard such terrible things.

Halloran gazed at him as if he were a strange specimen.

"So this is Bompard," he sneered. "This is our bold and brave little Bompard who double-crosses his customers and hobnobs with the Bolshevists. How now Bompard? How do you feel?"

"Oh, monsieur—" whimpered Bompard.

Halloran poked a toe into his ribs.

"Shut up," he said in conversational tone. "You will be attended to, Bompard. How much money can you raise against a sight draft on your bank in Marseilles? Speak the truth, you rat, or it will be bad for you. If you do lie it will be known, because you are going to remain in my power for some time to come. Now then, how much? Shall we say half a million francs?"

"It—might—be—possible," chattered Bompard.

"You poor fool," returned Halloran. "Do you think you are going to get away with half a million valueless francs? Do you think we have spent thousands of pounds for you to pocket? Do you think you are sitting in at a child's game? Your figure is four million francs, Bompard, and you'll get every sou of it no matter if you have to soil what scrap of soul you have left to got it. Bring him up, Rymer, and we'll get the draft made out."

It was a bad time for Bompard before he finally put his name to that draft. There were other papers, too, that had to be made out, for in order to raise the amount he had to send a power of attorney to his avocat in Marseilles to sell certain real estate. But Rymer and Halloran were adamant, and two days later the documents went by mail boat.

It was a week before a cable came announcing that matters had been arranged. It was then that Bompard thought he would at last be free. But not so. Rymer and Halloran had not yet finished with him.

"He'll get one lesson that he will remember," insisted Rymer; and Halloran agreed.

It was on a dark night that Bompard was put into a small boat and taken across to an Arab dhow that was just about to pass through the canal on her way to the Persian Gulf.

It was one of those mysterious craft under Halloran's control, and

Bompard was to go as one of the crew for a period of six months. At the end of that time, if he survived it, he would be free to take himself back to Marseilles.

As a matter of fact, Bompard did survive it and is once again in the brokerage business in Marseilles. But one thing he will not touch—no, not if you offer him a million francs gold. He will not have anything to do with charter-party business. Which goes to prove that lessons do sometimes prove salutary.

Incidentally these activities of Rymer and Halloran explain why it was that on his return to Marseilles, Sexton Blake was unable to find Monsieur Bompard in order to complete certain formal transfer business with him. He managed it, however, through Bompard's avocat, who held a power of attorney, but the avocat could not or would not explain the whereabouts of Monsieur Bompard.

THE END.

[41400 WORDS]
[I have now read just about 10% of Teed's works. This particular magazine issue is a little outstanding for the extent of the supplementary articles—they are usually restricted to one or two pages—the issues usually being exactly 64 pages inside the covers./drf]

" . . . two tons of the pure metal, worth, as I have said, four hundred thousand or more."

[Today that value would be $82 million US. The price today is $1277 per ounce. In 1927 it was $20.67 an ounce.]

Following:

The Great Cup-Tie!

by Anon.

CHAPTER 1.   The Stolen Banknote.

IN the office of James Ferrers, solicitor, of Crighton, the great football enthusiast, two clerks met one Saturday morning.

These were, respectively, James Wills and Albert Buchanan, and both were members of the local club, which was just about to start its season, and which, on the advice of Mr. Ferrers, had been entered for the Association Football Cup, that blue riband of the football world.

Wills, a smart young fellow, fair, and not bad looking, played forward for the club; Buchanan, a dark and sinister-looking man, helped his comrades at full back. The two were, both in physique and temperament, as different as it is possible for men to be.

Buchanan on this bright morning was troubled, as could be seen by the expression of his face. There was no one else in the outer office at the moment, and Wills, just entered from the street, was about to pass into the inner room when Buchanan stopped him.

"Wills, old man," said the latter, "I want a word with you."

"What is it about, old chap?" was the reply.

"Jim," said he, turning, "I want you to lend me a five-pound note!"

"Why, whatever for?" cried Wills. "You don't mean to say that you are hard up? Why, only this summer the governor advanced your salary."

"I know—I know!" cried Buchanan intensely. "My salary is good enough for any man to live upon. It isn't that. It is the cursed horses, Jim. I've lost again and again, until I am now in serious trouble, and unless you can help me out of it, it means ruin!"

"You've been betting again," said the younger man scornfully. "Well, you're a fool for your pains. You know if Mr. Ferrers heard of it he would sack you on the spot. He doesn't hold with that sort of thing."

Albert Buchanan turned aside his sinister face. His hands clenched convulsively.

"For mercy's sake, Jim!" he cried, "let me have the note. The governor will be here presently. He will unlock his cashbox, he will prepare the money for the bank, he will find that there is a five-pound note short, and—"

Jim Wills stepped back in horror.

"You mean, Bert," he cried, "that you took a fiver from the box?"

There was a moment of silence.

"I couldn't help it," blurted out the elder man at length "I had a strong tip sent down to me from the training-stables. You know what cursed luck I have had all the season. I went a plunge on it. I was certain the beast would win the race. I wanted to make up my losses. I saw the cashbox open when I entered Mr. Ferrers' room yesterday. He had gone to the private door with Lord Howe. I thought there would be no harm in borrowing a fiver for a few hours. I didn't think the horse could lose. I took it. But the horse did lose, and— Well, you see what it means to me, Jim. You won't see me ruined, will you? You'll help a pal in distress, won't you?"

There was a pause.

"Well, Bert," said Jim, after a long think, "I don't want to see you come to harm, though you deserve it right enough. Theft is a serious thing. Here you are! Here's a fiver. Put that back. And go straight after. Promise me you won't bet again!"

He was about to leave the room, when Buchanan stopped him again.

"Jim," he said, "there is something else I want you to do. I want you to put this note back in the cashbox."

Jim wavered. "Why should I mix myself up with this dirty business?" he asked himself. Then he looked at his fellow-clerk's face, which was rendered hideous by its look of despair.

"Give me the note," he cried, "and I will do it."

The next moment Mr. Ferrers came in, and Jim Wills, following him into the private office, found himself busy with a hundred tasks.

It seemed ages before he got the chance of placing the fiver in the cashbox. Mr. Ferrers would not leave the office. There was the cashbox upon the table, and as yet the money had not been counted over and prepared for the bank. Jim became as anxious and as nervous as if he were himself the guilty man.

At last Mr. Ferrers rose to leave the room. But he paused at the door.

Jim could bear it no longer. He must take his chance now he decided.

Quickly taking the fiver out of his pocket, he stretched across the table, and stuck the folded note well down amongst the others in the open box.

Alas! he had been watched. Mr. Ferrers' movements had been but a ruse to tempt him to betray himself. Like a flash the solicitor wheeled round.

"So. Wills," he cried, "it is you who are the thief! I could never have believed it!"

"I didn't take the money, sir," said Jim, with conviction. "I placed it back in the cashbox, I admit. But I didn't take it!"

The clerk's tone made Mr. Ferrers think awhile.

"If you didn't steal the money, then," said he, "you must know who did, seeing that you returned it. It must be one of the clerks in the office. Who was it?"

"I can't say, sir," said Jim, flushing again.

Mr. Ferrers turned in anger.

"The money was taken yesterday some time," said he, "and it was futile for the thief to think to return it without being detected. I had the numbers of all the notes, and this one that you have replaced" —he took it out and examined it— "does not tally with that of the stolen note at all."

He rang the bell fiercely. In response to the summons, Albert Buchanan entered. His face was pale beneath its tan.

"Buchanan," said Mr. Ferrers sternly, "do you know anything about a five-pound note being taken from my cashbox?"

The wretched clerk trembled, started; then, commanding himself with an effort, cried:

"No, sir!"

He would not look at Jim Wills.

"Well," the solicitor went on, "a note has just been returned by Wills to the cashbox from which the other note was stolen yesterday; but he says he did not take it."

Buchanan felt that he was in a ticklish position. Temptation came to him—temptation to clear himself at any cost, even by sacrificing the friend who had helped him.

"I know, sir," said he, with trembling voice, "that Wills did steal the note. I was about to enter this office yesterday morning when I saw him take it from the cashbox!"

Jim Wills uttered a cry at this, and reeled back.

"Sir," he cried, "this is too much! I did not intend to speak, but now I will, and without reserve. It was Buchanan who stole the note. He backed a horse with it yesterday, thinking he would win, but lost. He was afraid of being found out, and asked me to lend him a note, and to put it in your cashbox without you seeing. I did it to try and save him. But now I don't care. That is the truth, and he must put up with it!"

Mr. Ferrers looked from one to the other. He didn't know which to believe, and the whole business disgusted him.

"Well," he said, "it is a dirty business; and I am sorry that two lads, in whom I felt a considerable interest, and who are, moreover, members of the Crighton Club, should be implicated in it. There is a lie somewhere. I would have pardoned the theft, but under these circumstances, I cannot. I shall give you both into custody, and the magistrate shall decide which of you is guilty. I don't believe either of you!"

He rang the bell again. This time the commissionaire, who was always on duty outside, entered.

"Fetch a policeman!" said Mr. Ferrers. And he himself stood before the door, determined that neither of his clerks should escape.

The officer arrived, and the charge was stated.

Jim Wills began to protest. But his master silenced him with a word.

"No, Wills," said he. "You can say what you've got to say from the dock."

The prisoners were about to be removed, when into the office strode a big, burly man, with handsome face and breezy manner.

"Hallo, boss!" said he to Mr. Ferrers. "What's up? Two of our players in custody? That's rather hot, isn't it? And how the deuce do you think we're going to win this afternoon without 'em?"

The speaker was Bob Wright, the captain of the Crighton Rovers Football Club.

"I don't know and I don't care!" was the reply. "My clerks are no good. That's what is bothering me. I hate thieves, and I hate liars."

"What have they done?" asked the captain in astonishment.

Then Mr. Ferrers told him the story.

"A pretty tale, isn't it?" said he at the end. "One of them is a thief, a liar—perhaps both!"

"And that man is Albert Buchanan," said Bob Wright, looking the Crighton full-back straight in the eyes. "Jim Wills has told you the truth, sir. I heard them talking it over this morning. I was about to enter the office when I saw Wills take the five-pound note out of his pocket and give it to Buchanan. Then Buchanan asked him for mercy's sake to help him out of his trouble by placing the note in your cashbox when you weren't looking!"

"It's a lie!" shrieked Buchanan— "it's a lie, Wright, and you know it!"

"It is no lie!" said the captain coolly. "And, if further evidence is needed, here it is?" And Bob Wright drew a crisp banknote from his pocket. "This is the note you gave to Power the bookmaker yesterday. I saw you give it him. He owed me a fiver, and gave the note to me. Mr. Ferrers, compare the number with that of the note you lost, and see if what I say isn't correct!"

The astonished Mr. Ferrers examined the note, compared it with his numbers, and found that it was indeed the identical note which had been stolen from his cashbox the day before.

"That's good enough," said he. "Constable, you need only take Buchanan with you."

With a howl of rage, Buchanan sprang at Bob Wright, his late captain.

"This is your doing, curse you!" he cried.

But Bob Wright threw him back, the policeman seized him, there was a sharp click, and he stood handcuffed and wretched, doomed to the prison.

CHAPTER 2.   The Riot in the Winter Palace Gardens.

AT the wane of the football season all interest was centred in the final tie for the Association Cup. The League Championship had been won, and the lovers of the game were free to think only of this great event.

Crighton Rovers and Millingford were famous the world over now, having in a single season struggled up from dim obscurity to the height of their ambition—the final for the Cup.

Amongst the crowd there was one who was delighted. But just released from prison, he had come down to swear away the luck of his old club.

The minutes fled on. It wanted some thirty seconds to time, and there was no prospect of Crighton gaining a goal.

Bob Wright closed with a Millingford forward and wrenched the ball from him. With a rush, he was away and off towards the Millingford goal, with a dash and determination that brooked no check. Whether Millingford thought that they could not lose, and relaxed their efforts as it wanted but a few seconds to time, will never be known; but, one after another, Captain Bob Wright beat the opposition, and, waiting till his centre-forward, Jim Wills, had got on one side, he centred the ball, driving it right to his comrade's feet. There was nobody now but the Millingford goalkeeper to beat, and there was every chance of the game ending in a draw.

The crowd saw this, and those who favoured Millingford set up a terrific shout of "Time! Time! Time!"

The referee had the watch in his hand and his whistle in his mouth, ready to blow it.

"Quick, Jim!" shouted Bob Wright.

And quick it was. As the goalkeeper rushed out to challenge the daring forward, Jim Wills sent in a hot shot, and the ball, spinning with unerring aim and tremendous force, found the centre of the net. A second later the whistle blew! What a deafening cheer went up! Crighton had saved the game by one second, hats went into the air at the most sensational thing known in football history, and thousands charged over the field towards the pavilion and the players.

Hurrah! Hurrah! Hurrah! Cheer after cheer!

But the friendly set were not destined to have it all their own way.

There were many in the crowd who had made up their minds that the game ought to have ended half a minute sooner, and these set up a cry of "Shame! Shame! Shame!"

Then there was a call for the referee.

"Kill him! Boot him!" cried some. "Out with him! It wasn't fair! Millingford won!"

Amongst this chagrined set was Albert Buchanan.

"Go for the referee!" he yelled.

And, using his immense strength, he forced a passage where others could follow, and soon a free fight was waging, which carried Buchanan and some of the malcontents near to the referee. The official, seeing his danger, was doing his utmost to get to the dressing-room, and the police, alarmed at the state of affairs, were trying to get to him to protect him.

But Buchanan meant mischief. He saw Bob Wright by the referee's side. To get at the one was to get at the other. He made a desperate effort, and drew near. Soon his lean and hungry fingers were within reach of the referee; and, catching the gentleman by his throat, he dragged him towards the crowd, who were eager to clutch him

"Here's the referee!" roared the ruffian. "Give it him, boys!"

But he reckoned without Bob Wright, who had recognised him, and who saw the referee's peril.

"No, you don't. Buchanan!" cried the panting player, still blowing from his exertions in the field. "Let go the referee, or it will be the worse for you!"

With a snarl, Buchanan did let the referee go, and faced round at his old captain.

"Well," he cried, "since you will have it, we'll take it out of you. It don't much matter which it is!"

And he squared up to Bob Wright. But the captain was in no mood for nonsense. He had never liked Buchanan, even before the man became a gaolbird.

With a blow full upon the mouth, he sent the villain backwards. Then he signed to the men behind him, who were still cheering wildly, and carrying the players onward.

"Lad's," he cried, "some of the boys mean mischief. Put the players down, and form round them and the referee. Look out! Here they come!"

And they did come. With angry cries, led on by Buchanan, they surged forward. Then the fight became general. The Crighton players, tired out as they were, had to use their fists— and use them with effect, too, if they wished to gain the dressing-room in safety.

Shrieks, cries, shouts, and calls for the police were heard on every hand. Bob Wright and Jim Wills kept hard by the referee's side, and so, pelted with tufts of torn-up grass and mould, they went onward yard by yard. Then, when everything seemed all over with them, there was a charge from the police, baton in hand, and the ground was cleared. Taking advantage of the moment, the players raced on to the dressing-rooms, and found security within.

Then, as Bob Wright sat undecided, in came an inspector of police, panting for breath.

"Captain," said he to Bob Wright, "you and your men had better make a run for the station, or I will not be answerable for the consequences. Take what things you can, and dress in the train."

It was good advice.

"Come along, boys!" cried Bob Wright. "Just catch your bags up, throw your clothes into them, and off we go!"

And off they did go, making their exit from the other side.

The Rovers found themselves much jaded and worn after the fierce fight for the final of the Football Cup.

Millingford were in much the same plight. And so Crighton went to Brighton for a breath of sea air before returning to the fight, and the opponents travelled north to Blackpool.

Mr. Ferrers, whose interest in the club had made Crighton what it was in the football world, journeyed also to Brighton, determined to stay there until the team travelled up to London again; for the replayed tie was arranged to take place on the Palace ground.

And so here were Bob Wright, Jim Wills, and the rest of the Crighton team, enjoying themselves at London-by-the-Sea two days before the date fixed for the replay. Bob felt that Crighton could not leave now, and Mr. Ferrers was of the same opinion. The team was fit; not one of the team suffered from any injury; and it was reported that one of the Millingford men was on the sick-list.

As evening drew to a close, Bob Wright, leaving the hotel where the team was staying, by Mr. Ferrers' advice, strolled along the front in the gathering darkness, and made his way onward up the rise towards Kemp Town.

He felt light and strong and free, as does a man when he is in the pink of condition. No thought of fear for the morrow was upon him, nor did he give any heed to Jim Wills' report that he had seen Albert Buchanan in the town.

"Jim must be mistaken," he said, as he walked. "He's always thinking of that rascal. Buchanan knows better than to show his face here. The police are on the watch for him. A ticket-of-leaver who creates strife as soon as he is out of gaol is a man they want in again; and he's not reported himself to the police, I hear. Bah! Hang Buchanan! I don't fear him, anyway."

And so, turning up his coat-collar, for the evening was chilly, he set out at a swinging stride for his walk to Rottingdean and back.

Little did the brave captain of the Crighton Rovers think that he was being shadowed; that he had been watched leaving the hotel; that a spy of Buchanan's was treading on his heels, only waiting for the chance to signal to that villain himself, who was lurking on the cliffs towards Black Rock, waiting, as he had waited for several nights now, for Bob Wright to come out alone.

That they would win the replayed tie he felt certain.

The surest way to prevent such a thing, he thought, would be to disable their captain. Bob Wright had saved Crighton in the last match, as he had saved them in many others during the season. He was a host in himself, and his absence from the game at the last moment would undoubtedly demoralise the team.

Waiting in the shadow of the cliff, the villain saw Bob Wright coming onward with swinging stride; he saw his hireling signal, and, hurrying away, he went on till he had joined some loafers, who, smoking with hands deep in their pockets, looked desperate enough for any act.

"The man you want is coming along now," said Buchanan, with an oath. "You know what to do. When I give the signal, set upon him, and don't let him 'best' you. Don't kill him, but make it impossible for him to play in the game on Saturday. Do you understand?"

"Yes, guv'nor," said one of the gang. "But before we do the work let us see the colour of your money. It isn't a nice job. Let's have something in advance."

There was no help for it. Buchanan drew out a pocket-book, took some notes from it, and handed them round, ten shillings to each man.

"There!" said he. "There will be as much again for you when the work is done!"

But he had shown a bundle of crisp banknotes, and the man's eyes glittered with greed. Where the villain had got them from he alone knew; that they had been gained by honest toil was impossible.

The next moment there came a whistle from along the cliff.

The whistle was from the spy.

Bob Wright strode ahead again, enjoying his walk as only an athlete can. But of a sudden there came another whistle. This time the Crighton Rover was on his guard. But it was almost too late. Out from the darkness sprang five men, and the spy who had loitered behind joined them at a run. They were heavy odds against Bob Wright, and the footballer knew it. Still, his sharp eyes glanced round without a trace of fear in their steady depths. He was seeking for a means of escape.

"Hallo!" he cried, thinking to gain time. "What do you want with me?"

They shuffled nearer and nearer, uttering no sound.

"Why don't you speak, you curs?" cried Bob, backing against a fragment of broken fencing.

"Now, lads," cried Albert Buchanan, "don't shirk your work! In at him, and give him one on the head! When he is down we can better think what we will do with him!"

Bob Wright recognised the voice.

"Why, it's you, Buchanan!" he cried. "I might have guessed. Well, I'll give you something to remember me by this time!"

And with a spring he leapt upon the burly ticket-of-leave man and bore him backwards. Buchanan was nothing loth, and fought like a madman; but he had not the strength of the Crighton captain, and soon, with a cry, he fell helpless, and the captain, taking him by the throat, shook him till his teeth chattered.

"You brutes!" roared the villain to his men, "what have I paid you for? Don't stand there and see me killed. On him, and do for him!"

With a howl the ruffians lurched forward. Bob Wright had got his blood up now, and as he let go Buchanan's throat and faced his enemies his eyes flashed dangerously. He would fight it out, he thought, and make the hirelings sorry they had ever interfered with him. Then, as he noticed that some of them were armed with heavy sticks, he thought of the final tie. Crighton must win on Saturday—

they must! Mr. Ferrers would be broken-hearted if anything happened to spoil the club's chances, and if he were rendered incapable of playing Crighton would probably lose.

Discretion, in this case, was the better part of valour.

"No," thought Bob Wright. "I won't fight now; I'll run. I must keep myself out of mischief, for the sake of the club."

"Now then," he roared to the set of scoundrels, "stand back there, unless some of you want to be badly hurt! I'll damage you if you don't give way. Stand back!"

And he prepared to fight his way through them. Then up upon his feet sprang Buchanan, enraged and capable of committing any crime.

There was a heavy stone lying upon the grass, and seizing this, he hurled it with all his force at Bob Wright. The captain saw the movement, and put up his arm to protect his head. The stone struck it. Catching his enemy by the shoulder, he exerted all his strength, and hurled him away towards the verge of the cliff. Buchanan staggered on the slippery edge, threw aloft his arms, then disappeared over the side, until nothing could be seen but his hands convulsively clutching at the tufts of grass. Right in amongst the blackguardly hooligans did the Crighton captain now spring. Left and right he struck out, scattering the men like ninepins; then taking to his heels, he set off at a run towards Brighton Town, whose glittering lights he could see ahead.

CHAPTER 3.   The Day Before the Big Match.

IT was the morning before the great match at the Crystal Palace—the replayed final tie. In the breakfast-room of the hotel at which the Crighton team were staying sat Bob Wright and his comrades, eating their morning meal. With Bob sat Mr. Ferrers and Jim Wells, all three being in the best of spirits.

"I can't say how glad I am that you got free of that hired gang of hooligans last night, Wright, my lad," said Mr. Ferrers. "Had you waited a second longer I have no doubt you would have been so injured that there would have been our best man short to-morrow. However, all's well that ends well, and the police will have Buchanan in custody ere the day is out."

Here his eyes strayed to the door. A tall, distinguished-looking man had entered. Removing his hat, this gentleman came forward briskly.

"Hallo! Here is Inspector Charles," Mr. Ferrers went on. "I suppose he has news already. Good-morning, Charles! Glad to see you. You are about early. Anything happened?"

The inspector turned to Bob Wright.

"You are Mr. Wright, I believe?" he said.

"That is my name, sir," was the answer.

"You were attacked by this man Buchanan and some other on the cliffs near to Black Rock?"

"I was," said Wright, wondering what was coming next.

"Can you tell me what you did? Will you tell me exactly what happened in the struggle, as far as you can remember?"

"Certainly!" said Bob; and he described the struggle minutely.

"You admit, then," said the inspector, "that when you threw Buchanan off the last time he staggered to the verge of the cliff? Can you say whether he fell over or not?"

"I don't know," said Bob slowly. "I was too busily engaged in fighting my way free to notice what the blackguard did!"

The inspector's face was stern now.

"I am sorry to say," said he, turning to Mr. Ferrers, "that this man Buchanan is dead!"

"Dead!" cried Bob. "Why, how did he die? Who killed him?"

"His body was found lying on the foreshore this morning," said the inspector, "at the exact spot where he would have fallen had he

122

dropped when you hurled him towards the cliff. The police have made a minute search of the ground. There is every sign of a struggle having taken place just as you described, Wright. It is a case of manslaughter; but I am sorry to say that you will be arrested, and you will have to face the charge!"

Into the breakfast-room came two policemen in plain clothes. They crossed to Bob Wright, and stood one upon each side of him.

"Robert Wright," said the inspector, "you are arrested on a charge of having killed Albert Buchanan at Black Rock last night. Whatever you may say now will be used as evidence against you!"

Bob Wright looked round him in despair.

"Sir," said he to Mr. Ferrers, "it is all up with the Cup now. We shall lose. But, boys" —here he glanced at his comrades— "when you are in the midst of the battle to-morrow, think of me, and fight your best and bravest. Win if you can, lads. I'm done. This is the last straw. But don't think that I killed that blackguard, boys. I didn't. But that's neither here nor there. They want me, and I've got to go." Here he signed to the inspector. "Take me away," he cried; "I'm ready!"

They led him from the room. The inspector went out last. At the outer door Mr. Ferrers stopped him.

"Charles," he said, "will it be possible to arrange for bail? I want that man free, if it is possible, no matter what it may cost. Can you arrange for me?"

"I am sorry," said the inspector, with a shake of his head; "this is hardly a case for bail, you know. The charge is a serious one. There are those who say there was bad feeling between Wright and Buchanan. We have no evidence that your captain was set upon by a band of men at all. If he met Buchanan upon the cliff, and in the fight that followed murdered him, it would be to his interest to say that a band of men set upon him. I have the evidence of the coastguard that there were no men upon the cliffs last night. It is a serious matter. However, for the sake of old times, Ferrers, I will do all that is in my power. Still, I hold out little hope!"

Ferrers returned to the breakfast-room with gloomy face and puckered brow. It was a bitter blow, when everything seemed going on for the best.

"Lads," he said, "you have lost your captain, but play up for all you are worth, and win the Cup if you can!"

There was a ready response, but it sounded hollow, and rang, as it seemed, the death-knell of the Crighton Rovers' chance.

Mr. Ferrers looked round.

"Hallo!" he cried. "Where is young Wills?"

"He left the room just after Wright's arrest, sir," said one of the players. "I don't know where he has gone."

CHAPTER 4.   Jimmy Wills Investigates.

WHAT had become of the celebrated centre-forward, the good-hearted lad who had never been known to desert a friend in distress, Jimmy Wills?

He had disappeared, but whither had he gone? After the arrest of his friend, he went out. In the street he overtook Bob Wright, who was walking dejectedly enough between his captors.

Jim stretched out his hand.

"Bob," he cried, "I'm sorry, old man; but cheer up. They can't hurt you, and they shan't hurt you. Now I'm going to see what I can do to help you. If there's a chance of getting you free by to-morrow, I'm going to take it!"

"What are you going to do?" asked Bob, returning the pressure of his chum's hand.

"I'm going to see if I can find some of those men who fought you last night. They know more about this murder—if murder it be—than they care to say. That's why they're hiding from the police; but I'm going to find them!" And with a final squeeze to give Bob courage, and a look of defiance at the inspector, Jim Wills went upon his way.

Up the hill towards Kemp Town he went, and from there on to the cliffs; nor did he pause until he came to the spot where the fight had taken place the night before.

No need to search for it. There was a coastguardsman pointing it out to a visitor, and Jim Wills paused. Following the pair, he went to the verge of the cliff. To be sure, here were marks in the chalk, and places where the grass had been torn up, showing that a struggle had taken place.

Jim Wills looked at everything with the keenest interest.

"And so," the visitor was saying to the coastguard, "they say that the captain of the Crighton Club, that is fighting for the Cup at the Crystal Palace to-morrow, murdered this man?"

"They have arrested him for it," said the coastguard, "and that looks black, don't it? It's hard on the club, though."

"Who found the body of the murdered man?" was the next query, and the coastguard pointed downwards.

"His body had fallen upon a projecting piece of rock, and so the tide did not touch it. Mad Earle, a sailor, found him, and brought me information this morning. I told the police."

"A sailor found the body? Where is he now?"

"I don't know," said the coastguard; "I wish I did. The police would like to know, too!"

The visitor gave the coastguard a piece of money, and they walked, talking, along the cliff.

Jim Wills gazed after them. And so he had already learned something. The body of Buchanan had been found by a mad sailor, and the sailor had disappeared.

That was strange. Jim Wills felt of a sudden that he would like to find this mad sailor. He walked after the coastguard, and reached him the moment after the visitor had left him.

"Say," said he, "I heard you referring to the tragedy of last night. You spoke of a mad sailor finding the body. Do you know the man?"

The coastguard eyed Jim keenly.

"I don't know that I ought to answer any questions," he said doubtfully.

Jim gave him half-a-crown.

"I think you ought," he said; "and I will tell you that I'm a friend of Bob Wright, who has been arrested for the crime. You will answer now?"

"Yes, I will," cried the coastguard; "I'll tell you anything you want to know!"

"Well. then, where does this mad seaman named Earle live?" asked Jim eagerly.

"His home is at No. 7, Long Cut, Newhaven," was the answer; "but you'll not find him there, young sir. The police have been watching the place all day for him. He disappeared as soon as he had brought me news of the dead body on the beach. They want to hear what he has to say."

Evening was now drawing on. Jim thanked the coastguard, and turning his face in the direction of Newhaven, started off at a brisk walk.

At the westward end of Long Cut a few desolate houses stood aloof from the rest. Amongst these was No. 7. Jim knocked and knocked, but no answer did he get to his summons.

Disheartened, he turned away. But he decided to wait and watch a bit. He walked along a muddy path towards some fields. Here of a sudden a weird figure of a man clad in rough seaman's garb started out of the gloom, and turning, fled. It seemed to Jim that the man had been watching No. 7.

The footballer had managed to obtain a glimpse of the face of the fellow, and from what he had heard from the coastguardsman, knew, this must be the mad sailor, Earle.

Jim rushed after him.

"What do you want with me?" he cried.

"I want," said Jim firmly, "to know more about the murder of the man Buchanan, whose body was found on the foreshore at Black Rock this morning by you, Mr. Earle. You have kept out of the way of the police, and know more than you care to say."

"I shall have to give it up," he moaned— "I shall have to, in any case! I can't pass the notes—I can't. And if anyone found Mad Earle with money they would be suspicious. I had better tell the whole truth."

"You had," said Jim grimly. "So tell it to me. Out with it! You saw Buchanan murdered. Who did it? Tell me, and let me clear my pal."

"I will tell all," groaned the man. "I wanted to, only the love of gain kept me back. See!" Here he drew from his pocket a roll of banknotes, which he rustled in his fingers. "I took these from the body of the dead. I thought to keep them. But I have seen the police watching my house, and know that I cannot."

"You took these from the body of the corpse," said Jim. "Now, my man, out with it, who killed Albert Buchanan? They have arrested my pal for the crime, but he is innocent. Who killed the wretch? Tell me, quick!"

The mad seaman gazed round in fear.

"I don't know but what they aren't watching me now," he said, shivering. "I saw it all. There were five or six of them, and they waited for the young man to come along the cliff. Then they set upon him. How he fought! They could do nothing with him. I shrank back behind a ledge of sand and chalk and saw it all. The man they attacked threw the one who was afterwards murdered over the edge of the cliff; but he caught on with his hands, and—"

"Yes, yes!" cried Jim Wills eagerly. "What happened then? Did the man come back again?"

"Yes!" cried the sailor excitedly. "He drew himself up. And what a scene there was then! The young man they had attacked was well on his way back to Brighton, running like a trained man. They could never hope to catch him. Then the man who was afterwards killed quarrelled with the others. He called them sneaks and cowards. They turned on him. They demanded money from him, which he refused to give them. They said he had banknotes upon him, and they wanted them. Then, as he refused, one of them called to the others, 'Come on, lads, let us take 'em!'

"Then they set on him. He fought hard, but there were too many. Then one of them beat him down with a piece of broken timber, and, as he fell, he tumbled over the cliff, and went down. I don't think they meant to kill him. And after he had gone there was a silence.

"Then when they realised that it was murder, they agreed that they would say nothing about it. The money could remain with the dead, they said. And they separated, and went away as quickly as they could.

Jim Wills' face was now aglow with hope. Bless the thought that had caused him to remain behind!

"And what of you?" he asked wildly. "Why have you kept out of the way of the police?"

The mad sailor fidgeted; then, after an effort, went on.

"When I saw them go," he said, "I felt curious to know whether the man they had hurled over the cliff was dead or not. I made my way down to the foreshore by a path from the cliff that I know well, and, after a search, I found him. He was lying, with the water rapidly coming near to him.

"I drew him up, and placed him on a portion of the rock that is never covered by the tide. Then I found that he was dead. I thought of the notes. Since he was dead, and would want them no more, I thought that I might as well make use of them. I found them in his pocket-book, with some loose gold. The money he had in his pockets I took as well. Then, just when I turned away, I saw Jim looking at me."

"Who is Jim?" asked Wills.

"He is my boy—my son," said the sailor. "He had witnessed the fight as well as me, and he had watched me go down to the beach. I made him swear that he would say nothing about what he had seen. I wandered about till morning came, then I went to Coastguardsman Bill and told him that the body was down below. Then I feared that I might lose the notes, and I kept away from home. When evening fell, and I wanted to get in, I saw the police watching for me. Then you came, sir. And now you know all."

"Then come along with me," said Wills, "and help me to get my chum free. We can do it in time, if you like. I shall want evidence to substantiate your own. Where is your boy Jim?"

The sailor put his fingers into his mouth and emitted a shrill whistle. In answer to the summons out of the gloom of the meadow emerged the figure of the boy.

"All right, father!" he cried. "Here I am!"

And there, too, were the police. Two constables came out of the darkness and approached rapidly.

"All right," said Wills, as they came up. "Mr. Earle was looking for you. He has evidence that will release my chum, Bob Wright. He and his son were witnesses to the murder last night!"

CHAPTER 5. How Crighton Rovers Won the Cup.

NEVER in the history of football had such a crowd assembled on any ground as was present at the Crystal Palace on the afternoon following Bob Wright's sensational arrest. There was but one topic of conversation—the murder of the ex-Crightonian, James Buchanan.

As for Mr. Ferrers, he was downcast beyond expression. With Wills and Wright absent, he could see nothing before the team but failure. The Cup would go to Millingford, and the ambition of his life would be still unfulfilled.

Dejected and utterly miserable, he took his place on the grand-stand. He could not bear to enter the dressing-room. Without Wright and Wills there, the place depressed him.

A telegram was given him now by a special messenger. He tore open the envelope.

It had been detained, seeing that it had been sent at nine that morning.

"Sensational development in the Buchanan mystery," ran the lines. "There are formalities to be undergone, but Wright may be in London in time to play this afternoon. Am doing all I can to that end.—CHARLES."

The telegram was from Inspector Charles. Mr. Ferrers crunched it in his hand. It was all very well, but of what use was it? It could not bring Bob Wright to the field in time. Here were the Millingford men coming out upon the ground to the cheers of thousands, and it was already five minutes after the advertised time for the start.

There was an ominous pause. Where were the Crighton players?

Mr. Ferrers stood up and gazed round anxiously. Then out from the dressing-room they came, pushing their way through the crowd of admirers

One, two, three, four, five, six, seven, eight, nine. That was all. They walked soberly to the centre of the field, and, with folded arms, watched the dressing-room. What was the matter? Why didn't the reserves appear?

Hallo! What was this? Out upon the grass sprang the well-knit figure of a young man, whose ruddy face beamed with joy and health. It was Jim Wills. He had come in spite of the fact that Ferrers had given him up as lost. The gentleman's heart beat wildly. If Wills was here, where, then, was Bob Wright?

130

Jimmy faced round, and held up his hand. It was evident that he wished to address the crowd. "Silence!" came the cry. "Silence! silence!" And there was a hush as of death.

"Gentlemen!" shrieked Jimmy Wills, addressing himself to the stands. "Captain Bob Wright has been released!"

There was a second's silence, then a great cheer went up, which caused the very ground to rock. The cheers lasted for several minutes.

"The murder of James Buchanan," Jim went on, "was witnessed by a seaman, who has proved that Bob Wright was innocent. The real murderers will be in custody before long. And here" —indicating the entrance to the dressing-room— "comes Bob!"

Cheer after cheer, and out on to the grass rushed Captain Bob Wright. The first thing he did was to grasp Jim Wills cordially by the hand. Then he went to the centre, the coin was spun. Crighton had won the toss, and before the spectators could realise the fact the ball was in motion.

Whether the sudden arrival of their dreaded opponent, Bob Wright, had demoralised the Millingford team—which had made up its mind that it would win—will never be known, but, with a rush, Jim Wills carried the ball down the field. Crighton swept on to the attack. They had the crowd with them now, and cheers burst forth as Jimmy pounded the ball into the goalkeeper's arms. The man kicked clear; but Bob Wright recovered the ball from a Millingford forward, and once more play ruled in the Millingford territory.

Jim Wills had the ball now. He played out to the right wing. The wing cleverly beat a Millingford back; the ball was centred again to Wills, and he, being charged by a halfback, back-heeled to Bob Wright. The Crighton captain made no mistake; in a stiff tussle he cleverly retained possession of the ball, and, with a spinning shot which curled along inches only off the ground, he beat the Millingford goalkeeper, and the sphere of leather trailed away into the netting unhampered.

A goal to Crighton, and the game scarcely begun!

Of what use is it to detail the match that is now a landmark in English football history? Crighton Rovers won the Cup, and won it handsomely, as all of us know.

THE END.

Shipping Thefts.
Our Magazine Corner.

People laughed when the Aquitania lost her anchor some little time back. "What a thing to lose!" many newspaper readers chuckled, as the news item met their eyes. "Fancy mislaying a 'little' thing like that!"

In this case it really was mislaid—or, rather, dropped accidentally. When the loss was discovered, divers fished it up again without too much trouble. But what about an anchor being stolen? There are shipping "rats" who make a speciality of this kind of theft, especially in out-of-the-way ports in South America and other countries where the docks are not watched and guarded with quite the same care and diligence as is exercised in British ports.

They will "lift" an anchor with the same ease which they would display in stealing the skin off a rice pudding. The business is organised to such an extent that the anchor is pinched and safely stowed in some rascally ship-outfitter's depot without the least suspicion being raised that the loss of the anchor might be due to anything but an accident in dock, such us the Aquitania experienced.

Where does the profit Come in? No, the missing anchor is not melted down. It is sold a bit later to another ship's master, who, arriving at the port after the departure of the vessel that "lost" it, finds his own anchor mysteriously gone, and has perforce to buy another one. No inconsiderable expenditure that!

His own anchor has been smartly "weighed" by the ship-outfitter's gang of "rats," and in turn will be sold to the next comer to replace the anchor stolen from him! So that the phrase "the anchor's weighed," has come to have a very different meaning from the original significance. To effect the theft it might be necessary to "treat" the watchman left aboard whilst the crew is ashore—treat him so generously that he soon loses all interest in the proceedings, and leaves the deck clear for the "rats" to do their job. But that's waste of money, say the crooks, when a sandbag or length of lead tubing will answer the same purpose just as well!

But the theft of an anchor dwindles into insignificance beside the theft of an entire ship. Not that the latter often "comes off" with the ease shown in the case of the 400-ton steamer Ferret, which was hired for a pleasure cruise in sunny seas. The man who hired the Ferret had a head on him, as the saying goes.

The steamer vanished cleanly off the face of the deep, the only trace of its existence being a couple of boats, ostensibly the Ferret's, bottom upwards, that were afterwards spotted bobbing about in the Mediterranean. There was ample evidence of the steamer's fate—a wreck! But the Ferret was still very much afloat.

The Ferret had meanwhile been rechristened. She sailed the seas as the Benton, and was now trading in comestibles. The Benton actually sold her first cargo to a dealer on the African coast —and then the man who had hired her, as the Ferret, tried to sell the ship, too! But there was nothing doing, so another cargo was taken aboard and another name adopted.

This time the Ferret was the India, and it was under that alias that she fell into the hands of the Melbourne Customs authorities, who, despite the new paint and various minor alterations which had been made in her appearance, recognised her as the supposedly wrecked Ferret. The stolen ship went back to the man who had hired it out, and the man who had hired it went to prison, along with his crew.

Before the London river police reached the highly organised and efficient state that they now rightly boast, the Thames was a positive happy hunting-ground for shipping thieves. Thousands of pounds' worth of merchandise disappeared each year, chiefly in the night, from the ships laying at anchor in the "Pool." That sort of criminal game has been practically stamped out. But the high seas, and the big ports of foreign countries, still offer scope for thieves who are blessed—or cursed—with a blimp of originality.

Even ships' captains sometimes join the ranks of shipping, thieves, co-operating with their rascally owners in casting away over-insured vessels. One such ship was wrecked purposely, with what was reputed to be a cargo of gold worth £400,000. The underwriters who had undertaken the insurance had the vessel raised—she had gone down in shallow water—and found that the cargo was not gold, but old iron!

That is the sort of crime that the intelligence service of Lloyd's, the "brain" of the shipping world, is for ever trying to defeat.

R/R

www.ingramcontent.com/pod-product-compliance
Lightning Source LLC
Chambersburg PA
CBHW052148170626
46812CB00004B/1643